THE whistle blew and the prisoners packed up and started to descend the scaffolding.

There was a press of men jammed together on the narrow platform which spanned the scaffolding at the third story. Brady was at the front and as he started to turn to go down the ladder backwards to the next level, a hand shoved him violently in the small of the back.

He went head first into space with a cry of fear and then someone grabbed at his denim jacket, jerking him to one side. His hands fastened over a length of scaffolding and he hung there for a moment before scrambling to safety under the rail.

The whole incident had taken place in a second.

It was no accident.

HELL
IS
TOO
CROWDED

by

Jack Higgins

FAWCETT GOLD MEDAL • NEW YORK

For my Grandmother
MARGARET HIGGINS BELL
with affection

HELL IS TOO CROWDED

THIS BOOK CONTAINS THE COMPLETE TEXT OF
THE ORIGINAL HARDCOVER EDITION.

Published by Fawcett Gold Medal Books, a unit of CBS Publications, the Consumer Publishing Division of CBS Inc., by arrangement with Harold Ober Assoc., Inc.

ISBN: 0-449-14274-4

10   9   8   7   6   5   4   3

(1)

TO Matthew Brady, caught between the shadow lines of sleep and waking when strange things fill the mind, the face seemed to swim out of the fog, disembodied and luminous in the yellow glow of the street lamp. Once seen it was not easily forgotten, wedge-shaped with high cheekbones and deep-set, staring eyes.

He was conscious of the wrought-iron frame of the bench hard against his neck, of the light drizzle beading his face. He closed his eyes and took a deep breath. When he opened them again he was alone.

A ship moved down the Pool of London sounding its foghorn like the last of the dinosaurs lumbering aimlessly through a primeval swamp, alone in a world that was already alien.

Somehow, it seemed to sum up his own situation. He shivered slightly and reached for a cigarette. The packet was almost empty, but he fumbled around for a while and finally managed to light one. As he drew in the first lungful of smoke, Big Ben struck two, the sounds curiously muffled by the fog, and then there was silence.

He felt utterly alone and completely cut-off from all other human beings. He leaned on the parapet under the lamp, looked down through the fog to the river, and asked himself what now? Only the foghorn of the ship on its way down to the sea answered him and it was as if it were calling good-bye.

He turned away, pulling up the collar of his jacket, and a woman ran out of the fog and cannoned into him with a gasp of dismay. She started to struggle and he held her at arm's length and shook her gently. "You're okay," he said. "There's nothing to worry about."

She was wearing an old trench-coat tightly belted at the waist and a scarf tied peasant-fashion about her hair. She looked about thirty, with a round, intelligent face, her eyes dark and troubled in the light of the street lamp.

For a moment, she gazed up into his face and then, as if reassured, laughed shakily and sagged against the parapet. "There was a man back there. Probably harmless enough, but he appeared so unexpectedly from the fog, I panicked and ran."

Her English was good, but with a slight foreign intonation. Brady took out his cigarettes and offered her one. "The Embankment is no place for a woman at this time in the morning. Some pretty queer birds doss down here for the night."

The match flared up in his cupped hands and she lit her cigarette and blew out a tracer of smoke. "You don't have to tell me. I only live across the road. I spent the evening with a girl friend in Chelsea. Couldn't get a cab, so I decided to walk." She laughed. "If it comes to that, you don't seem the type for a bench on the Embankment yourself."

"It takes all kinds," he said.

"But not your kind," she told him. "You're not English, are you?"

He shook his head. "Boston, Massachusetts."

"Oh, an American," she said, as if that explained everything.

He managed a tired grin. "Back home I've got friends who'd argue with you on that one."

"Have you far to go?" she said, "or do you intend spending the night here?"

"I'm not even sure how I got here," he said. "I've a room at a hotel near Russell Square. I'll make it all right in my own good time."

Heavy drops of rain spattered down through the branches of the sycamore trees and he pulled the collar of his jacket tightly around his neck, feeling suddenly cold. The woman frowned. "Look, you ought to be wearing a coat at least. You'll catch pneumonia."

"Any suggestions?" he said.

She took his arm. "You can walk me home. I'm sure there's an old raincoat hanging in the cupboard back at my flat. You can have it."

He didn't bother to argue. All the strength seemed to have drained out of him and the moment he started to walk, the fumes of the whisky seemed to rise into his brain again.

The fog pressed in on them, pushed by a finger of wind, and they crossed the road and walked along the echoing pavement. Rain dripped steadily from the branches of the trees and a car swept past, invisible in the fog, as they turned into a side street.

He noticed the name high on the wall of the corner house on an old blue-and-white enamel plate—Edgbaston Gardens—and in front of them, the fog seemed to be tinged with a weird orange glow. A nightwatchman's hut loomed out of the darkness and at the side of it, a coke fire flared in an iron brazier.

Brady caught a brief glimpse of a dim figure sitting in the hut, face faintly illuminated by the fire. "Be careful!" the woman warned. "There's a guard rail somewhere about here. They're doing something to the gas main."

He followed close behind her as she skirted iron railings and then mounted some steps to a door and fumbled for a key in her handbag. The house was the end one in the terrace and at the side of it stretched a graveyard, a church tower shadowy in the night.

It all seemed transitory and unsubstantial as if it might fly away into the fog at any moment and Brady followed her hurriedly into the hall and waited for her to switch on the light.

An old Victorian wardrobe stood against the wall at the bottom of the stairs and in its mirror, he saw a door open behind him and caught a brief glimpse of a face, old and wrinkled, long jet ear-rings hanging on either side. As he started to turn, the door closed quietly.

"Who's your neighbour?" he said.

She frowned. "Neighbour? The downstairs flat is empty so you don't need to worry about noise. I'm on the first floor."

Brady followed her upstairs, clinging to the banisters and feeling curiously light-headed. No one could expect to shrug off a two-day jag just like that, but there was a strange dream-like quality to everything and his limbs seemed to move in slow motion.

The door to her flat was at the head of the stairs and she unlocked it and led the way in. It was surprisingly well furnished. Thick pile carpet covered the floor and concealed lights gently illuminated rose-tinted walls.

He stood in the centre of the room and waited. She took off her coat and scarf and ran her hands over close-cropped dark hair as she moved forward. He swayed slightly and she placed her hands on his shoulders, bracing herself to support him.

"What's wrong?" she demanded anxiously. "Aren't you well?"

"Nothing that a jug of coffee and a good night's sleep won't cure."

She was warm and desirable and very close. Suddenly, all the anger and frustration of the past two days seemed to drop from his shoulders like an old cloak. There was, when all was said and done, only one real cure for his condition. He pulled her close and kissed her gently on the lips.

For a moment she responded, and then she pushed him firmly away, down into a large padded chair.

"I'm sorry," he said.

"Don't be silly." She went to a cocktail cabinet which stood against the far wall, mixed a drink, and brought it back to him. "A hair of the dog. Drink up! It'll do you good. I'm going to make coffee. Afterwards, I'll get some blankets. You can have the divan."

Before he could protest, she had crossed the room to the kitchen and he sighed and leaned back, allowing each tired muscle to relax.

Whatever she'd put in the drink, it was good—very good. He took it down in two easy swallows and reached for a cigarette. The pack was empty, but there was a silver box on a coffee-table on the other side of the room.

He got to his feet and suddenly, the room seemed to stretch into infinity and the coffee-table was at the wrong end of a telescope. He took one hesitant step forward and then the glass slipped from his nerveless fingers.

He was on his back and the woman was bending over him. She looked completely calm and unperturbed and behind her, the door opened and then closed again.

The face of the man who appeared at her shoulder, was wedge-shaped with deep-set, staring eyes, a face from a waking nightmare that Brady had last seen looming out of the fog above him on the Embankment.

He opened his mouth in a soundless scream of warning, and then the room seemed to spin round in a whirl of coloured lights, sucking him down into darkness.

(2)

PAIN, exploding in a chain reaction, brought him back from darkness as someone slapped him repeatedly across the face. There were voices near by, a confused and meaningless blur, and then a tap was turned on.

His head was forced down by a strong hand and he choked as ice-cold water surged into his nostrils. The pressure was released and he breathed again, but only for a moment. His head was pushed back down relentlessly. When he was dragged upright again, there was a roaring in his ears and he could hardly breathe, but his vision was clear.

He was in a small, white-tiled bathroom and his reflection stared out at him from a waist-length mirror. His face was haggard and drawn, the eyes deep-set in their sockets, and there were scratches down one cheek.

His shirt was soaked in blood and he leaned on the

washbasin for support and stared at himself in bewilderment. A thick-set man in shabby raincoat and soft hat stood at his shoulder, eyes hard and unsympathetic in a craggy face.

"How do you feel?" he demanded.

"Lousy!" Brady croaked, and the voice seemed to belong to a stranger.

"That's good, you bastard," the man said and pushed him roughly through the door.

The living-room seemed to be crowded with people. A uniformed constable stood by the door, and two plain-clothes men worked their way round the room, dusting for fingerprints.

A tall, thin man with grey hair and horn-rimmed spectacles, sat at one end of the divan with a notebook and listened to a small, bent old man, who stood before him twisting a cloth cap nervously between his hands.

As Brady moved forward, the little man saw him and an expression of fear crossed his face. "That's him, Inspector Mallory," he said. "That's the bloke."

Mallory turned and regarded Brady calmly. "Are you quite sure, Mr. Blakey?"

The little man nodded confidently. "I'm not likely to forget him, governor. Saw him plain, standing in the doorway when she switched on the light."

Mallory looked tired. He made a note in his book and nodded. "That's fine, Mr. Blakey. You go back to work. We'll get a statement from you later."

The little man turned away to the door and Brady said slowly, "Look, what the hell's going on here?"

Mallory looked up at him coldly. "Better show him, Gower," he said.

The detective who had brought Brady from the bathroom, pushed him across to the bedroom. Brady hesitated in the doorway. There was a flash and a photographer turned and looked at him curiously.

The room was a shambles, the floor was littered with toilet articles from the dressing-table and the curtains fluttered in the breeze from the smashed window. The bedclothes trailed down to the floor and the far wall was etched with a delicate spray of blood.

Another detective was on his knees wrapping an antique whalebone walking-stick in a towel. It was slippery with blood and he turned and looked across the room and suddenly, there was silence.

Gower pushed Brady forward to the end of the bed. Something was lying there draped in a blanket, squeezed between the bed and the wall.

"Take a look!" he said, pulling the blanket away. "Take a good look!"

Her clothes had been ripped and shredded from her body. She sprawled there wantonly, her thighs spattered with blood, but it was the face which was the ultimate horror, a sticky, glutinous mess of pulped flesh.

Brady turned away, vomit rising into his mouth, and Gower cursed and shoved him across to the door. "You gutless wonder!" he said viciously. "I'd like to string you up myself."

Mallory was still sitting on the divan, but now he was examining Brady's passport. Brady looked down at him, horror in his eyes. "You think I did that?"

Mallory tossed Brady's jacket at him. "Better put that on; you might catch cold." He turned to Gower. "Stick him in the other bedroom. I'll be along in a minute."

Brady tried to speak, but the words refused to come and Gower hustled him across the room, through the bathroom and into another bedroom. It was small and plainly furnished with a single divan under the window and a fitted wardrobe in an alcove. Gower pushed Brady down on to a small wooden chair and left him in the care of a young constable.

When the detective had gone, Brady said, "Any chance of a cigarette?"

The constable hesitated and then unbuttoned his tunic and took out a battered silver case. He gave Brady a cigarette and a light without speaking, and returned to his post by the door.

Brady felt tired, really tired. The rain beat against the window and the cigarette smoke tasted of dead leaves and nothing made any sense. The door opened and Gower and Mallory came in.

Gower moved across the room quickly, a scowl on his face. "Who the hell gave you that?" he demanded, plucking the cigarette from Brady's mouth.

Brady tried to stand up and the detective hooked a foot in the chair and pulled it away, sending Brady sprawling to the floor.

Brady came to his feet, anger rising inside him. This was something tangible, something he could handle. He hit Gower hard beneath the breastbone and as the detective doubled over, lifted his right into the man's face sending him back against the opposite wall.

The young constable drew his staff and Gower scrambled to his feet, face contorted with rage. Brady picked up the chair in both hands and retreated into a corner.

As they advanced towards him, Mallory said sharply from the doorway, "Don't be a fool, Brady!"

"Then tell this big ape here to get off my back," Brady said savagely. "If he lays a glove on me again, I'll pound his skull in."

Mallory moved in between them quickly. "Go and get cleaned up, George," he told Gower. "Make a cup of tea in the kitchen—anything. I'll send for you when I need you."

"For Christ's sake!" Gower said. "You saw what he did to that girl."

"I'll handle it!" Mallory said, and there was iron in his voice.

For a moment longer, Gower glared at Brady, and then he turned quickly and left the room. Brady lowered the chair and Mallory nodded to the constable. "Wait outside."

The door closed behind the constable and Mallory took out a packet of cigarettes. "You'd better have another," he said. "You look as if you could do with one."

"You can say that again," Brady told him. He accepted a light from the inspector and slumped into a chair.

Mallory sat on the divan. "Perhaps we can get down to some facts now."

"You mean you want a statement?"

Mallory shook his head. "Let's keep it on an informal level for the moment."

"That suits me," Brady told him. "To start with, I didn't kill her. Didn't even know her name."

Mallory took a photo from his pocket and handed it

across. "Her name was Marie Duclos, born in Paris, been living over here for about six years." He took out a pipe and started to fill it from a leather pouch. "A known prostitute. After the Act chased her off the streets, she did what a hell of a sight too many of them have done—got herself a flat and a telephone—or someone got them for her."

The photo was old and faded and Brady frowned and shook his head. "It doesn't look much like her."

"That's not surprising," Mallory said. "If you look on the back, you'll see it was taken when she was eighteen and that's ten years ago. You'd better tell me how you met her."

Brady told him everything, just the way it had happened, from his first awakening on the Embankment, to the events in the flat.

When he had finished, Mallory sat in silence for a while, a slight frown on his face. "What it really comes down to is this. You maintain you saw a man on the Embankment in the fog who you later saw again, here in this flat, standing behind Marie Duclos, just before you passed out."

"That's about the size of it."

"In other words, you're implying that this man committed the murder."

"He must have done."

"But why, Brady?" Mallory said gently. "Why pick on you?"

"Because I was here," Brady said. "I suppose it could have been any poor sucker she happened to be entertaining."

"But if he *was* here, where did he go afterwards?" Mallory said softly. "You and the woman were the only people to use the front door all night. The night-watchman swears to that."

"How did you know something was wrong here?" Brady said.

Mallory shrugged. "The nightwatchman heard her scream and then a candlestick was thrown through the window. He knocked them up next door and asked them to ring for us. He still had the door under observation the whole time. Nobody left."

"There must be a rear entrance."

Mallory shook his head. "There's a yard and an overgrown garden with a six-foot fence of iron railings dividing it from the graveyard."

"It's still a possibility," Brady said. "And what about the old girl downstairs? Maybe she saw something?"

"The downstairs flat hasn't had a tenant for two months now." Mallory shook his head and sighed. "It won't do, Brady. For one thing, you told me you first saw this man on the Embankment *before* the Duclos woman spoke to you. Now that just doesn't make sense."

"But I couldn't have killed her," Brady said. "Only a madman could have beaten a woman to death like that."

"Or a man so drunk that he didn't know what he was doing," Mallory said quietly.

Brady sat there, staring helplessly at him. The whole world seemed to be closing in on him and there was nothing he could do about it—nothing at all.

The door opened and the young constable came in and handed Mallory a slip of paper. "Sergeant Gower thought you might find this interesting, sir."

The door closed behind him and Mallory quickly scanned the paper. After a while he said, "It would appear that you're a pretty violent man when the mood takes you, Brady."

Brady frowned. "What the hell are you getting at?"

"We've just run a quick check to see if anything was known about you. Since flying in from Kuwait three days ago, you seem to have spent the intervening time in trying to drink yourself into an early grave. On Tuesday night you had to be ejected from a pub on the King's Road after knocking down the landlord who refused to serve you because of your condition. Later that night, you were involved in a fight in a drinking club in Soho. When the bouncer tried to throw you out, you broke his arm, but the owner refused to press charges. You were finally picked up by the police in the Haymarket at four a.m., drunk and incapable. It says here that you were fined two pounds at Bow Street yesterday. Quite a record."

Brady got to his feet and paced restlessly across the room. "O.K., I'll tell you about it."

He stood looking out of the window, down into the street, watching the policemen standing under the street lamp, their capes shining with rain.

"I'm a constructional engineer. Work mostly on bridges and dams and that sort of thing. I met a girl in London last year called Katie Holdt. She was German, working for some family over here as a children's nurse while she learned the language. I fell pretty hard, wanted to marry her, but I was short of cash."

"And what was your solution?" Mallory said.

Brady shrugged. "There was an opening in Kuwait

—a new dam. The money was exceptional as nobody wanted the job. Working conditions were pretty grim, mainly because of the heat. I took it on, lived off the company for ten months and had my salary credited to Katie here in London."

Mallory looked pained. "And the usual thing happened, I suppose?"

Brady nodded. "I flew in three days ago after ten months of hell and discovered from her employer that she'd returned to Germany a month ago to get married." He slammed a balled fist into his palm. "And there was nothing I could do about it—not a damned thing. It was all legal."

"And so you decided to get drunk," Mallory said. "So drunk, you didn't know what you were doing for most of the time."

Brady shook his head deliberately. "O.K., Inspector, so I got drunk. I even got mixed up in a couple of brawls, but I didn't kill that woman."

Mallory got to his feet. He crossed to a small dressing-table, picked up a mirror and held it out. "Take a look!" he said. "Take a good look!"

The blood from the scratches had dried and they looked ugly and somehow sinister. Brady touched them gently with his fingertips. "You mean she did that?" he said in a whisper.

Mallory nodded. "The doctor took blood and skin from underneath the fingernails of her right hand. He'll examine you when we get down to the station."

Brady clenched his hands to keep them from shaking. "I'm an American citizen. I'd like to get in touch with my Embassy."

"That's already been taken care of," Mallory said, opening the door into the bathroom.

Brady made one more try. He paused in the doorway. "Let's go over this thing again, Mallory. There's got to be an answer somewhere."

"There's only one thing might help you now, Brady," Mallory told him, "and that's a lawyer. I'd ask your Embassy to get you a good one. The best there is. You're going to need all the help you can get."

Gower was standing outside and his eyes glittered malevolently as Brady moved past him. They took him downstairs and paused at the top of the steps while Gower produced a pair of handcuffs.

It was still foggy and the rain bounced from the asphalt surface of the street in solid rods. Several police cars were parked in the road and a small group of curious people crowded along the railings, held back by a couple of constables. It looked as if most of the inhabitants of the quiet street had turned out, probably awakened by the unaccustomed noise of the cars.

As Gower clamped one steel bracelet around the American's wrist, Brady stiffened suddenly. Standing out from the mass of faces was one he was already only too familiar with. In the same moment, its owner melted into the fog at the rear of the crowd and disappeared.

Brady pulled away from Gower and jumped down into the crowd, the handcuffs swinging from one wrist. He burst his way through and then someone stretched out a foot and tripped him so that he fell heavily. As he started to get up, they were upon him.

Gower twisted his arm and Brady turned desperately as the inspector came forward, "I saw him, Mallory," he said. "He was there at the back of the crowd watching. He can't have got far."

In the light of the street lamp, Mallory looked suddenly more tired than ever. "For God's sake, cut it out, Brady! This isn't going to get you anywhere."

Brady's control snapped completely. He lifted an elbow into Gower's face, tore free, and plunged through the crowd, striking out madly at the faces which surrounded him.

It was no good. He pulled away from the clutching hands and turned with his back to the railings. "Come on!" he cried. "Come and get me, you bastards!"

They came in a rush, Gower leading the way. Brady smashed a fist into the detective's face and then a staff cracked down across his right arm. He swung again with his left. Someone twisted it behind his back and they forced him down against the wet flagstones. He cursed and kicked out wildly.

It took six of them to get him into the car.

(3)

THE governor of Manningham Gaol sighed. Men who had been in the condemned cell always seemed to have that look about them—as if the whole world was their enemy. On the other hand he'd always considered it rather barbaric to let a man sweat it out until the appointed day was almost upon him before reprieving him. It was hardly to be wondered that anyone who had gone through such an experience should be different from other men.

It was eight o'clock in the evening and he was already late for a bridge party. He shuffled the reports neatly together, replaced them in their file, and leaned back in his chair.

"This is a maximum-security prison, Brady," he said. "There's no way out except through the front gate. That's why men are sent here. You'll find that most of the inmates are serving long sentences or life, like yourself. Have you any questions?"

"No, sir!" Brady said.

The light from the desk threw his face into relief. It had fined down in the past three months and there was a touch of grey in his hair. His eyes were cold and hard and devoid of any expression. He looked a thoroughly dangerous man and the governor sighed. "I understand you attacked a prison officer while on remand at Wandsworth? I wouldn't advise that sort of thing here."

"I was under great stress at the time," Brady said.

The governor made no comment, but opened the file again. "You were a constructional engineer by profession, I see. We'll be able to make use of you. We're building our own extensions, within the walls, of course. There's no reason why you shouldn't start in the morning with the others."

"Thank you, sir!" Brady said.

"Of course, I need hardly mention that it's a privilege which will be revoked at the first sign of bad behaviour. Do I make myself clear?"

"Perfectly, sir!"

The governor smiled briefly. "If you feel in need of advice at any time, Brady, don't hesitate to see me. That's what I'm here for."

He got to his feet as a sign that the interview was over and the chief officer led Brady out.

Manningham was the third prison Brady had been in during the past three months and he looked about him with interest as he was taken to the clothing store, then to the kitchen for a meal, and finally to his cell.

The building had been constructed in the reform era of the middle of the nineteenth century on a system commonly found in Her Majesty's Prisons. Four, three-tiered cell blocks radiated like the spokes of a wheel from a central hall which lifted 150 feet into the gloom to an iron-framed glass dome.

Each cell block was separated from the central hall by a curtain of steel mesh for reasons of safety, and the chief officer unlocked the gate into C Block and motioned Brady through.

They mounted an iron staircase to the dimly lit top landing. The whole place was wrapped in an unnatural quiet and the landing was boxed in with more steel mesh to stop anyone who felt like it, from taking a dive over the rail. It gave one a feeling of being in a steel labyrinth and Brady shivered slightly as the Chief paused outside the end door on the landing and unlocked it.

The cell was larger than he had anticipated. There was a small barred window, a washbasin and fixed toilet in one corner. Against one wall, there was a double bunk, against the other, a single truckle bed.

A man was lying on the single bed reading a magazine. He looked about sixty, white hair close-cropped to his skull, eyes a vivid blue in the wrinkled, humorous face.

"New cell mate for you, Evans," the Chief said. "He'll be joining the gang on the building site tomorrow. Show him the ropes." He turned to Brady. "Remember what the governor said and watch your step. Play fair with me, and I'll play fair with you."

The door closed behind him with a slight clang and the sound of the key turning in the lock seemed to carry with it all the finality in the world.

"Play fair with me and I'll play fair with you." The man on the bed snorted in disgust. "What a load of crap." He sat up and produced a twenty packet of cigarettes from under his pillow. "Have a fag, son. My name's Joe Evans. You'll be Brady, I suppose?"

"That's right." Brady took a cigarette. "How did you know?"

Evans shrugged and gave him a light. "Got it on the vine from Wandsworth. Hear you tried to do a screw down there?"

Brady lay on the bottom bunk and inhaled with conscious pleasure. "He needled me from the day they got me in there on remand. I couldn't take any more."

"Those Sunday papers gave you a rough time, didn't they?" Evans chuckled. "I expected you to have fangs and two heads."

In spite of himself, Brady grinned, and Evans smiled back at him. "That's the way, son. Don't let the bastards get you down. If you ever feel really depressed, spit right in some screw's eye. It can always be guaranteed to liven things up."

"I'll bet it can," Brady said. "What's it like here?"

"Better than some. They'll be sticking some other bloke into that top bunk soon, but you've got to expect that these days. I came here three years ago when they made it a maximum-security nick for bad lads. There hasn't been a single crash-out since then."

"How long have you got to do?"

The old man grinned. "That's up to the Board. I've served six years of a seven-stretch. Would have been out by now if I'd minded my manners to start with." He blew smoke up in a long plume to the ceiling. "Not to worry. My old woman's got a nice little guest house going in Cornwall. They won't see me back here again."

"I seem to have heard that one somewhere before," Brady said.

"But I mean it," Evans said. "I'll tell you something, son. You know what ruined me? Being too good at my bloody job. When I blow a safe, it makes no more noise than a mild belch. Trouble is, I do it so expertly, the cops always know where to come."

"You seem to have things pretty well organized here anyway," Brady said, holding up his cigarette.

Evans grinned. "I'm not complaining. You fell on your feet, getting in with me, son."

"What's this building work the governor was telling me about?"

"They can't cope with the crime wave, so we're having to build 'em another cell block in the main yard. It's a good number. Better than sewing mailbags or sitting on your fanny in here all day going slowly nuts. Should last another ten months if we take it easy."

"I don't intend to be around that long." Brady stood up and went and peered out of the window. The outer wall was perhaps forty feet high and the main railway line ran on the other side of it. Beyond, through the autumn night, the lights of Manningham gleamed fitfully. They might as well have been on another planet.

"Now look, son," Evans said seriously. "Don't beat your head against a stone wall. That's the way to end up in the other place. Nobody can crack this can. I've been here three years and I tried every possibility. There's no way out."

Brady turned and looked at him. "But I've got to get out. I was framed, Evans. Somebody else battered

(26)

that girl and used me as a fall guy. I want to know who and why."

"The story you told at the trial was one thing," Evans said. "It was a good try, but it didn't work. We're all guilty in this place. Guilty of getting caught."

Brady shrugged helplessly. "Sometimes I think I must be the only sane person in a world gone mad." He walked across to the door and touched it lightly with his fingers. "If only I could open this for a start."

Evans stood up and crossed to the cupboard under the washbasin. He opened it and took out an ordinary spoon. "Always happy to oblige."

He pushed Brady out of the way and knelt down in front of the door. The lock was covered by a steel plate perhaps nine inches square. He quickly bent the handle of the spoon and forced it between the edge of the plate and the jamb. He worked it around for a few moments and there was a click. He pulled and the door opened slightly.

"God Almighty!" Brady said.

Evans pushed the door gently into place and worked the spoon round again. There was another slight click and he stood up.

"But that's incredible," Brady said.

Evans shook his head. "An old lag's trick. Plenty of geezers in this place can do as much. Most of these doors are mortice deadlocks, fitted years ago. One of these days they'll get wise and change them." He grinned. "Not that it would matter much. Show me any key you like for five seconds and I'll copy it from memory."

He went back to his bed and lit another cigarette.

"But I don't understand," Brady said. "You told me it was impossible to crash-out of this place."

The old man shook his head pityingly. "Have another fag, son, and let me tell you the facts of life. Getting out of this cell is only the start. You've got to get through the cell-block gates downstairs. That puts you in the central hall. From there you've got no less than five gates to pass through before you hit the yard, and the main entrance is a fort by itself. Even the governor has a pass." He shook his head. "This is maximum security, son. Some of the worst bastards in the business are doing time here. That's why they converted the place."

"I'll find a way," Brady said. "Just give me time."

But it's got to be soon, he said to himself as he lay down on his bunk. It's got to be soon. I can't take much more of this. He closed his eyes and the face seemed to smile at him out of the darkness, the face that had stayed with him through his trial and the two weeks as a walking dead man in the condemned cell.

Why me? he asked himself. Why me? But there was no answer, could be no answer until he got out of this place and found one. He turned his face to the wall, hitched a blanket over his shoulders and drifted into a troubled sleep.

The days that followed merged into a pattern. Each morning after breakfast, fifty men paraded for the chief officer in the main yard and were allocated their work for the day. The main fabric of the building was already in an advanced state of construction, but there was still a considerable amount of work to do on the steel framework of the fourth storey.

Evans had been working as a welder and riveter up there and Brady was placed in his charge. After seeing the skill with which the American handled a blow torch, the old man sat back and let him get on with it.

"By God, son," he said. "What I could teach you to do with that torch is nobody's business. You're a natural."

Brady grinned and pushed his goggles up from his eyes. "You're incorrigible, you old hellion. You'll come to a bad end yet."

Evans gave him a cigarette and they crouched down in a corner between crossed girders and looked out over the town. It was a crisp autumn day, the air tinged with a hint of the winter to come. Beyond the gaunt chimneys of the grimy Yorkshire industrial town, the moors lifted in a purple swell, fading almost inperceptibly into the horizon.

"By God, it's good to be alive on a day like this," Evans said. "Even in here."

Brady nodded and glanced briefly down into the main yard below, watching the men working on the brick pile below with the duty screws hovering near by. There could be no illusion of freedom there, not with those dark uniforms standing out so clearly.

He looked across at the glass dome of the central tower and his eyes followed the fall pipe that dropped forty feet to the roof of D block. The block branched out from the central tower like a pointing finger, and stopped thirty or forty feet from the perimeter wall. He sighed and flicked his cigarette end out into space. A man would need wings to get out of this place.

Evans chuckled. "I know what you're thinking, son, but it just isn't possible. You're in a privileged position because it's all spread beneath you like a map. If you can find a way out, I can get you five hundred quid for the information any time."

"Maybe I'll hold you to that." Brady picked up his torch. "Let's get back to work."

For the next two weeks he kept his thoughts to himself, but each day, working high on the extension, he used his eyes until finally, every detail of the prison buildings was imprinted on his brain. It would take careful planning, but already there was the glimmering of an idea at the back of his mind.

Just before noon on Thursday, a duty officer called him down and told him he had a visitor. As he waited in the queue outside the visiting room, Brady wondered who it could be. He had no friends in England and both his parents were dead. There was only his sister in Boston, and she had been over already for the trial.

When his turn came, the duty officer took him in and sat him in a cubicle. Brady waited impatiently, the conversation on either side a meaningless blur of sound, and then the door opened and a young girl came in.

She was perhaps twenty, her dark hair close-cropped like a young boy, the skin sallow over high cheekbones, the eyes dark brown. She was not beautiful, and yet in any crowd, she would have stood out.

She sat down hesitantly, looking rather unsure of herself. "Mr. Brady, you won't know me. My name is Anne Dunning."

Brady frowned. "I'm afraid I don't understand."

"You knew my father, Harry Dunning," she said.

"I believe you worked together on the Zembe Dam in Brazil."

Brady's eyes widened and he leaned forward. "So you're Harry Dunning's daughter. How is he? I haven't heard from him since we parted company in New York after finishing the Zembe job. Didn't he go to Guatemala?"

She nodded, hands twisting her purse nervously. "He's dead, Mr. Brady. Died in Coban six weeks ago after a bad fall."

Brady was genuinely shocked. "I'm sorry to hear that," he said awkwardly. "Your father was a good friend of mine."

"That's exactly what he said about you," she said. "I flew out as soon as word reached me of his accident. I was with him for two days before he died. He'd heard about your trouble. He told me you could never have done such a thing. That you must have been telling the truth. He said you once saved his life."

"It's nice to know that somebody believed me," Brady said.

She opened her purse and took out an old-fashioned silver watch and chain. She held it close to the gauze screen so that he could examine it. "He wanted you to have this. He asked me to see that you got it personally. I suppose I could give it to the governor to put with your other things."

He shook his head gently. "It's no use to me here. You keep it for me."

"Would you really like me to?" she said.

He nodded. "I might be out of this place sooner than you think, then you'll be able to give it to me personally."

She slipped the watch back into her purse and leaned forward. "But I understand they'd turned down your appeal?"

"Oh, I've got a few things working for me." He smiled, dismissing the subject. "Tell me about yourself? How did you know where to find me?"

"There was a bit in the newspapers when they moved you," she said. "I'm with a show playing Manningham Hippodrome this week. It seemed like a good opportunity. I telephoned the governor this morning and he said it would be all right."

"How's business?" he said.

She grimaced. "Terrible. We're supposed to be on a twelve-week run of the provinces, but I think we'll fold on Saturday night." She sighed. "I really thought I'd got a break this time. A good second lead and three solo spots, but that's show business for you."

"I'd give a hell of a lot to be sitting slap in the middle of the front row tonight when you come on," Brady said.

Her eyes crinkled at the corners and she smiled warmly. "And I'd give a lot to have you there, Mr. Brady. I think my father was right. Do you think they'll let me come and see you again before I leave Manningham?"

He shook his head. "I'm afraid not, but you could write."

"I'd like to do that," she said. "I'll let you have my London address."

The duty officer touched him on the shoulder and Brady stood up. For a moment she just stood there, looking at him through the gauze and it was as if she wanted to speak, but couldn't find the words. She turned abruptly and went out and he followed the duty officer down to the dining-hall, thinking about her all the way.

When they paused for a smoke back on the job that afternoon, Evans quizzed him about her. "Who was she, son? I hear she looked pretty good."

"Is there anything you don't hear?" Brady demanded.

Evans grinned. "If there is, it isn't worth knowing."

Before Brady could think of a suitable reply, the whistle blew signifying the end of work for the day and they packed up and started to descend the scaffolding.

There was a press of men jammed together on the narrow platform which spanned the scaffolding at the third storey. Brady was at the front and as he started to turn to go down the ladder backwards to the next level, a hand shoved him violently in the small of the back.

He went head first into space with a cry of fear and then someone grabbed at his denim jacket, jerking him to one side. His hands fastened over a length of scaffolding and he hung there for a moment before scrambling to safety under the rail.

The whole incident had taken place in a second and the majority of the men hadn't even noticed it. Brady leaned against the rail and wiped sweat from his face as Evans pushed through the crowd towards him. "I've never moved faster," he said.

"Did you see how it happened?" Brady asked.

Evans shook his head. "There was a hell of a push back there at the top of the ladder. Everyone was in such an all-fired hurry to get down."

"I guess I was lucky you were on hand," Brady told him.

But the thought stayed with him, the niggling doubt. A hand had pressed him squarely in the small of the back and pushed outwards into space, of that he was certain. But why? He had made no enemies and his friendship with Evans alone assured him of a privileged position amongst the other prisoners.

He thought about discussing it with Evans, but decided to let it go. He had more important things on his mind. Much more important.

That one omission proved almost fatal. On the following morning, just before noon, he was working on the third-storey catwalk welding a fractured pipe. Behind him, bricks were hauled by hand in a canvas bucket to the fourth storey.

It was pure chance that saved him. He pushed back his goggles to pause for a breather, and out of the corner of one eye, caught a quick flash of something coming towards him. He dropped flat on his face, and the loaded bucket swung lazily out into space over the end of the catwalk, and back again.

He glanced up as it was hauled over the edge of the catwalk above him by a tall, swarthy individual with a broken nose and dark, curling hair. The man returned his gaze calmly for a moment and then walked away.

Brady went up the scaffolding hand-over-hand to the fourth storey, where he found Evans welding angle irons in one of the half-completed rooms at the north end of the building.

The old man pushed up his goggles and grinned. "Time out for a smoke?"

"Someone just tried to make me take a dive off the third storey," Brady told him.

Evans stood up slowly. "You sure?"

"It's the second time in two days," Brady said. "That business at the top of the ladder yesterday afternoon was no accident."

"Got any ideas?" the old man asked.

Brady nodded. "Come outside and I'll show you."

The man with the broken nose was loading a wheelbarrow with bricks at the other end of the catwalk.

Evans frowned. "That's Jango Sutton. Fancies himself as a bit of a tearaway. Doing a seven-stretch for robbery with violence. Clobbered a seventy-year-old nightwatchman with an iron bar. A real hard man," he added sarcastically.

"He looks like a foreigner," Brady observed.

Evans shook his head. "He's a diddy-coy—a gipsy. Lives here in Manningham as far as I know. Married a local girl."

"I'd like to know who put him up to it."

Evans nodded grimly. "That's easily handled. You get him in here and leave the rest to me."

Sutton wheeled the load of bricks along the catwalk and they went back inside the room and waited. As the gipsy passed the doorway, Brady reached out, grabbed him by the scruff of the neck, and pulled him inside with such force that Sutton staggered across the room and hit the opposite wall.

"Here, what's the bloody game?" he demanded, getting to his feet.

"You've tried to make me take a dive twice in two days," Brady said. "I want to know why."

"Get stuffed!" Sutton replied and ran for the door.

Evans stuck out a foot and tripped him and the gipsy sprawled on his face. As he twisted and started to get up again, Evans shoved him down with one foot and squatted beside him, the blow-torch in one hand. He adjusted the flame until the steel tip glowed white-hot and grinned wolfishly.

"We only want you to be reasonable, Jango."

The gipsy licked his thick lips and gazed in fascinated horror at the tongue of flame. "You wouldn't dare."

"But I'll be doing you a favour," Evans said. "Five seconds of this on your kisser and you'll be able to put Boris Karloff out of business when you get out. They won't need to make you up."

"You're mad!" Sutton said and his voice cracked slightly.

"I will be if you don't tell us what we want to know," Evans told him and suddenly, his voice was cold and hard and utterly ruthless. "You'd better start talking, boy. Who put you up to giving my pal here a push off the catwalk?"

Sutton shook his head from side to side and tried to crawl away backwards. Evans grabbed him by the shirtfront with his free hand and advanced the torch.

Sutton struggled madly, his face contorted with fear. "I'll tell you," he said hysterically. "It was Wilma—my wife. She came to see me yesterday morning. Told me there was five hundred nicker for me if I saw that Brady met with an accident. An extra two-fifty if it happened by Sunday."

Brady stood in the doorway, one eye on the catwalk

outside in case a screw turned up. "Who put her up to it?" he demanded urgently.

"I don't know," Sutton replied. "She wouldn't tell me."

"He's lying," Brady said. "It doesn't make sense."

Evans pulled Sutton upright and held the torch so that the heat started to singe the gipsy's black hair. "It's the truth," Sutton screamed. "I asked her who was behind it, but she wouldn't tell me."

Evans glanced up at Brady. "Satisfied?"

The American nodded and Evans pulled Sutton to his feet and held him close for a moment. "You put a foot wrong from now on, boy, and I'll see you get sliced from here to Christmas."

He shoved Sutton away from him and the gipsy twisted like an eel under Brady's arm and out of the door. Evans turned off the torch and took a couple of cigarettes from his jacket pocket. "Can you make any sense of it?"

Brady shook his head. "Do you know anything about his wife?"

"Keeps a drinking club down by the river," Evans told him. "It's called *Twenty-One,* and anything goes, believe me. She's been on the game since she was four-teen."

Brady lit his cigarette and stood by the door, a frown on his face. After a while, Evans said, "What's running through your mind now, son?"

"A lot of things," Brady said. "For example, the fact that somebody's got a vested interest in seeing me dead. I'd like to know why. If I can find out, I think it'll give me the answer to a lot of things including who killed Marie Duclos."

"And what are you going to do about it?" Evans said shrewdly.

Brady turned and grinned. "You've got a nose like a ferret." He went across to a pile of rubble and bricks in one corner and pushed a hand down the back and pulled out a coil of manilla rope. "There's forty foot there," he said. "And a six-foot sling that fastens with spring links. I've had them here for a week now and there's a pair of wire-cutters hidden in my mattress. That's all I need."

"All you need for what?" Evans said, frowning.

"I'm crashing-out," Brady said. "I've got a lead now—Wilma Sutton. I'll find out who put her up to this business if I have to beat it out of her."

"You're crazy," Evans said. "It can't be done."

"Anything can be done if you put your mind to it," Brady said. "Come up top and I'll show you."

They went out on to the catwalk, climbed up the scaffolding and squatted in an angle of the steel framework. "You were right when you said that getting out of the cell didn't achieve anything," Brady said. "Nobody could ever hope to get through all those gates and guards. I've decided to cut them all out."

"How the hell do you plan to do that?" Evans demanded.

Brady nodded towards the glass dome of the central tower. "Have you ever noticed the screw turning a handle by the entrance to our cell block in the central hall? A system of wire pulleys goes right up into the dome and opens a ventilating window there. That's the way I'm going."

"You must be crazy!" Evans said. "That central tower is all of 150 feet."

"It can be done," Brady told him. "I'm going to cut my way through the steel mesh at the end of the landing. From there I can reach part of the iron framework which supports the tower. It goes right up into the dome."

"Nobody could climb that lot," Evans said. "Those beams are nearly perpendicular. It can't be done."

"It can by someone with specialized experience," Brady told him. "Don't forget I was a structural engineer. I've worked on bridges and tall buildings all over the world. I'll wear rubber shoes and use the sling with the spring links as a safety belt."

"Let's say you get out through the dome," Evans said. "Then what?"

"There's a fall pipe drops down to the roof of D Block." Brady nodded across. "I can crawl along the roof ridge to the chimney of the laundry. From there, I'll rope down to an iron pipe that runs across to the perimeter wall. It's the one really weak link in this place, but I figure they must think it's harmless. Nobody could reach it from the ground. It's forty feet up."

"And forty feet across," Evans said. "Even if you got that far, you'd still stand a fair chance of breaking your neck."

"I'm going," Brady said stubbornly. "Nothing's going to stop me."

Evans sighed. "When are you thinking of trying?"

"Sunday evening," Brady said. "It's dark by five and we're locked up for the night at six. From then on, there's only one duty screw who works from the central hall, checking all blocks."

"That could be dodgy," Evans said. "He usually pussyfoots around in carpet slippers. You never know where he's going to hit next."

"I'll take my chance," Brady said. "With luck, they might not find I'm missing till breakfast time. I'll need you to do the necessary with that spoon, of course."

Evans grinned. "You'll need me for more than that. Let's say you get over the wall and into the town. What are you going to do for money and clothes?"

Brady shrugged. "Break in somewhere. Take my chances. What else can I do?"

"I've got a key I made for myself in the machine shop," Evans told him. "It's hidden back in the cell. Opens any mortice deadlock known to man." He grinned. "Well, almost any. If you can get over the wall, cross the line to that churchyard over there. On the other side, you'll find a little lock-up shop. One of these surplus places. You can outfit yourself there. If you're lucky, you might even find a float in the till."

"Are you sure about that?" Brady said.

Evans nodded. "Remember I told you how I tried to find a way out of here when I first arrived? A bloke in my cell put me on to the shop. That's why I made a key. It was a perfect set-up, but I could never find a way out. Now, it's too late."

Brady turned and looked out across the wall to the railway line and the churchyard beyond. The shop and the key were the final touch. He felt completely calm, completely sure of himself.

It was only after the noon whistle when he was following Evans down the ladder that his hands started to tremble slightly because he was crashing-out and nothing was going to stop him.

(4)

RAIN lashed against the window as Brady peered out into the darkness. After a while he turned round and grinned tightly. "It's a hell of a night for it."

Evans was standing at the door, listening. He turned and nodded. "That's it, son. If you're going, go now."

Brady lifted his mattress and pulled out the coil of rope which he looped over one shoulder. The sling went round his waist, the wire-cutters into his pocket and he was ready.

Evans was already on his knees at the door. A moment later there was a click and it opened slightly. The old man peered out cautiously and then turned and nodded. "Have you got everything?"

Brady clapped him on the shoulder. "There's only one thing I'm worried about. What might happen to you."

Evans grinned. "I've never been so surprised in my

life as when you opened this door, and they couldn't expect me to grass, now could they? As much as my life's worth." Brady tried to think of something adequate and Evans grinned again. "Go on, son. Get to hell out of it, and good luck."

The landing was dimly lit and the whole block wrapped in quiet. Brady stood there for a moment and then, as the door closed behind him, he moved quickly and quietly in his rubber shoes to the stairs at the far end.

Only a single light illuminated the hall below and the dome itself was shrouded in darkness. He balanced on the rail and clawed his way up the steel mesh curtain until he reached the roof of the cell block. He quickly hooked the snap links of the sling to the wire, securing himself in place and then took out the wirecutters and got to work.

It was surprisingly easy and he took his time cutting first in a straight line across the roof and then down the side of the wall, link by link. It only took him five minutes and when he had finished, he slipped the wire-cutters into his pocket and pushed the section he had cut outwards.

The first steel beam lifted from a ledge in the wall of the hall about three feet to the right. He unclipped the spring links of his sling and reached out carefully through the opening. He could barely touch the beam. He took a deep breath and pushed himself forward. For a moment, the wire mesh held him and as it started to sag, he secured a firm grip on the edge of the beam. A moment later, he was standing on the ledge, wedged between the beam and the wall.

A gate clanged down in the hall and he held his

breath and waited. The duty officer passed through the pool of light and stopped at his desk. He made an entry in the night book and then continued to A Block on the far side. He opened the gate, locked it behind him, and disappeared.

Brady lost no more time. The sling went round the beam and then his waist. He snapped the spring links together, leaned well back, bracing himself against the sling, and started to climb.

It was really no worse than some of the construction jobs he had worked on, he told himself. That bridge in Venezuela, for instance, high in the Sierras, with the winds blowing men from their perches like flies every week, had been infinitely more dangerous. The only difference was that he'd been paid for doing that— well paid.

He conquered an insane desire to laugh and looked down. The patch of light had receded, had grown infinitely smaller. It was as if the prison itself was falling away from him and he took a deep breath and moved on.

On several occasions he had to unhook his crude safety belt as he came to cross girders, but it was only as he moved towards the edge of the dome itself that he experienced any real difficulty.

The beams curved round, hugging the wall for the last ten feet or so, and there was only an inch or two behind them where he might push one end of the sling. That he would fail to attempt it never really entered his head. He looked down from his perch on a cross beam, down to that tiny patch of light below, and then forced one end of the sling behind the beam and snapped the links into position.

The first couple of feet weren't too bad, but as the cupola started to curve, his body inclined outwards. He forced his feet hard against the beam and leaned his weight against the sling. Inch by painful inch he moved up until his body was seemingly arched out in a bow and he knew that if he dropped back his head the merest fraction, he would be able to look straight down at that light below. Once, his foot slipped and the sling creaked ominously. His bowels turned to water. He braced his feet desperately, moved another six inches in one try, and reached up and over the ledge.

His fingers groped about desperately and finally fastened over a ridge of metal. He hung there, delicately balancing himself with one hand, and with the other, carefully unhooked the sling.

Just as deliberately, he secured it about his waist. His body started to swing outwards. He reached up with the other hand, doubled his grip on the ridge of metal, and heaved himself up on to the ledge.

He lay there for a moment, breathing deeply, his hands shaking a little. There was enough room only for his body squeezed against the curved glass panes. The ventilating window was on the other side and he started to crawl cautiously round.

The ledge was thick with the dust of the years and it drifted down into the gloom, filling his nostrils, making him want to sneeze badly.

The window was closed. He tried to push it open, but it refused to budge and he took out his wire cutters and severed the wire line which curved round the cupola down to the hall below. He held on to the severed ends and doubled them carefully over the metal catch, and then he pushed the window open and crawled out on to the ledge outside.

The view was magnificent and the lights of Manningham gleamed through the curtain of rain. A train passed along the track, its whistle echoing through the night and he breathed in the freshness and was filled with a fierce delight.

The fall pipe was the original Victorian one, square and sturdy and nailed against the wall as firmly as if the builders had intended it to serve the life of the building.

He went backwards over the edge without a thought, hung for a moment from the square box at the top, and started to descend, his fingers moving easily in the gap between the pipe and the wall.

It took him little more than a minute to reach the ridge of D Block. There was a car standing outside the gate office in the yard below. A duty officer came out and leaned down to the window. A moment later he signalled and the gates started to open and the car drove out. Probably the governor going to one of his Sunday night bridge parties. Brady grinned involuntarily. The bastard would have something to occupy himself with tomorrow.

He moved easily along the ridge of the roof, a foot on either side, hands braced on the tiles. The laundry chimney was still warm and he moved to one side of it and peered down.

He couldn't see a damned thing. He remembered Evans's words about getting this far and still having a better than even chance of breaking his neck, and shivered slightly. He pushed the thought away from him and squatting against the wall, quickly uncoiled the length of manilla.

In a way, this was the trickiest part of the whole operation. He couldn't tie the rope to the chimney because he needed it to descend the outer wall. He passed one end round and for a moment, stood there, bracing himself, the double strands firmly gripped in both hands, and then he went over the edge.

His feet slipped against the wet brickwork and he swung against the wall, skinning his knuckles, and his legs bumped painfully against the pipe.

He sat on it, legs astride, back against the wall, and pulled on one end of the rope and it snaked down through the night. He coiled it quickly, slipped it around his neck, and started to inch his way across the pipe.

For those remaining minutes, time seemed to come to a stop and all sounds were muted as he moved through the almost total darkness. It seemed like a dream to him when he reached out with one hand, touched rough stone, and looked up to see the edge of the wall, a dark line against the night sky.

He quickly uncoiled the rope, fastened one end around the pipe and tossed the other over the wall. His fingers hooked into a tiny crack in the stonework and he stood up.

The edge of the wall was comfortably within his reach. He pulled himself up, carefully negotiated the rusty iron spikes and slithered down the other side. He dangled at the end of the rope for a moment before dropping six feet into wet grass at the top of the railway cutting.

He was soaked to the skin and as a train approached, he lay down and turned his face into the wet grass, heart pounding painfully. When it had passed into the distance, the sound of it still trembling on the damp air, he got to his feet and slithered down the bank without even a backward glance at the wall behind him.

As he crossed the track and scrambled up the bank on the other side, a clock struck the half-hour. Twenty minutes from leaving his cell—that's all it had taken. Unless anything went wrong, that gave him twelve hours before first rounds in the morning.

He went over the low wall into the churchyard and moved cautiously between the gravestones. Light showed in the tall windows and an organ played the opening bars of a hymn. A moment later the congregation joined in, their voices rising into the night.

He decided that evening service must be just starting. He kept to the wall all the way round to the gate and slipped out.

It was a poor neighbourhood, the streets lined with dilapidated terrace houses and the shop stood on the corner only twenty or thirty yards away. A van swished by, tyres hissing on the wet asphalt, and then there was silence.

As he crossed the street, he had the key ready in his hands. His stomach was suddenly hollow and for the first time, he was afraid. Perhaps Evans had been wrong. Perhaps the key wouldn't fit the lock?

He moved into the dark entrance of the shop, hesitated for the merest fraction of a second, and then bent down. His groping fingers found the lock, the key turned smoothly. A moment later, he was standing inside, his back to the door, shaking with reaction.

There was a door behind the counter and he moved round quickly and opened it. A small window looked out into a dark backyard and he drew the curtain and switched on the light.

The room was crammed with stock from floor to ceiling. Most of the stuff looked second-hand and he quickly found a serviceable tweed suit and selected a pair of shoes from a pile in one corner. He found the other things he needed on the shelves.

There was a basin in one corner with a mirror above it and he quickly examined himself. The face of a stranger looked out at him, skin stretched tightly over the cheekbones, hair plastered against his skull.

There was only a cold-water tap, but he stripped and washed the dirt from his body, towelling himself down briskly afterwards. The suit fitted as well as could be expected and when he was dressed, he pushed his prison garments under a pile of second-hand clothing in one corner and went back into the shop.

Evans had been right. There was a float in the till. Three pounds in ten shilling notes and two in silver. He slipped the money into his hip pocket, selected a cheap trench-coat from a rack and found a hat on one of the counters. It was a size too large, but slanted over one ear it looked presentable.

He moved across to the door and opened it. There was no sound. He locked it gently and walked away along the street at a brisk pace and the sound of the singing from the church faded into the night behind him.

The rain hammered down and he turned up his collar and paused to get cigarettes and matches from a machine. The cigarette tasted different, something to do with being free, he decided, and felt suddenly alive for the first time in months.

One advantage of working on the building extension at the prison had been the fact that it had given him a fairly good idea of the layout of the town. He walked through the empty streets in the general direction of the river, finding *Club Twenty*-One with surprisingly little difficulty after inquiring the way from a youth waiting on a corner for his girl.

It was situated in a cobbled street leading down to a barge dock, an old converted house on the corner of an alley. There was a cheap, neon sign over the entrance and the board said members only. Brady pushed open the door and went in.

The corridor was long and dark with dirty, brown walls and a faintly unpleasant smell. An old, white-haired man in a faded blue uniform edged with tarnished braid, sat in a glass cubicle under the stairs, reading a newspaper.

He glanced up and pale, watery eyes examined Brady dispassionately. "Members only, sir!" he said in a light colourless voice.

Brady leaned in at the window and smiled. "I'm only in town for the night. A friend of mine told me that *Twenty-One* was a good place to have a little fun."

"You've got to have a sponsor, sir," the old man told him. "That's the law."

Brady took out a ten shilling note and smoothed it

between his fingers. "That's a real pity, especially as I'm only going to be in Manningham tonight."

The old man coughed and put down his newspaper. He pulled forward a ledger and handed Brady a pen. "Under the circumstances I can't see as how it would do any harm, sir. You'll have to pay the pound membership fee, I'm afraid."

"Happy to pay it," Brady said. He signed the book in the name of Johnson and gave the old man three ten shilling notes. "Where do I go now?"

"Top of the stairs sir. Just follow the sound of the music." Brady went up to the first floor quickly. At least he was inside. From now on he would have to play it by ear.

There was a small cloakroom at one end of the corridor and a young, badly painted girl of no more than sixteen polished her nails and looked bored.

She took Brady's coat and hat and gave him a ticket. "Is Wilma in tonight?" he said casually.

The girl nodded. "Having a drink at the bar when I was in five minutes ago."

The main room of the club had been constructed by knocking down the dividing walls of several smaller rooms. The place was crowded with tables and chairs, leaving only a postage-stamp dance floor and the music came from a large and brassy juke-box in one corner.

As yet, it was early in the evening, and the place was virtually empty. Two couples danced, another sat at a table, drinking.

Brady went towards the bar. He could see himself coming in the mirror and the suit looked surprisingly good. The barman leaned against the wall, polishing glasses. He looked like a Cypriot or Greek with crisply curling hair and a pretty-boy face.

Brady ordered a double brandy to create an impression and looked deliberately across at the woman who sat on the far curve of the bar, reading a magazine. "Ask the lady if she'll have a drink with me," he said.

"You drinking, Wilma?" the barman asked her.

She looked up and examined Brady calmly and critically. After a while she smiled. "Why not? I'll have a Pimms, Dino."

Her hair was a blonde halo and she walked round the bar and stood six feet away from him, a hand on her hip. "Do I know you?"

Her pose was studied and deliberate, he realized that. She looked as if she didn't have a stitch on under the black sheath dress and was proud of it. Her breasts were sharply pointed and beautifully formed, the stomach faintly rounded, legs long and tapering to delicate ankles.

She was one hell of a woman—almost perfect. It was her face which spoilt the picture; sensual, coarse and vulgar, the eyes cold and calculating and full of cunning. The face of an animal.

He grinned. "No, this is the first time I've been to Manningham."

She slid on to the stool beside him, exposing a generous length of leg. "That's funny, I could have sworn I've seen you somewhere before. You're an American, aren't you? We get a lot of Americans in here. There's an Air Force station only a few miles out of town."

"I've been up here on business from London," he

said. "I'm going back in the morning. Thought I might find myself a little fun before leaving."

"Well, we'll have to see what we can do, won't we?" She finished her drink and slid off the stool. She smoothed the dress over her rounded hips and smiled invitingly. "Like to dance?"

They threaded their way between the tables as someone put a coin in the juke-box and it started to play a soft dreamy number with a saxophone wailing somewhere in the background.

Wilma melted into Brady's arms, moulding her supple body into his, and slid an arm up behind his neck. As they moved slowly round the tiny floor, Brady tightened his grip, pulling her against him.

"Heh, watch it! I break easily!" she said.

He grinned down at her. "What do you think I'm made of—stone?"

"You tell me," she said.

He had been apart from women for so long that it was easy to play the role. He caressed her back with one hand and whispered urgently. "For God's sake, Wilma, isn't there somewhere we can go?"

"Sure there is," she said calmly. "But it'll cost you."

"Then let's go," he said.

She walked ahead of him, out into the corridor and down to the far end. Another flight of stairs lifted into the darkness to the second floor. Brady followed her up and she opened a door and led the way into a well-furnished bedroom.

The walls were painted in pastel shades of blue to contrast with the pink carpets. The only furniture was the large divan bed which stood against the wall, a small table beside it on which stood a telephone.

Wilma turned off the main light and clicked another switch and concealed wall lights cast a subdued glow over the room. Brady stood just inside the door and she closed it, turning the key in the lock, and put her arms around his neck.

Whatever else one could say about her, she certainly knew her business. When she kissed him, her mouth opened and something seemed to crawl up his spine. He crushed her against him, returning the kiss avidly.

After a moment, she pulled away, breathless and laughing. "Let's have a smoke," she said. "We've got plenty of time."

He gave her a cigarette and she sprawled on the bed, her head against the pillow. "The more I look at you, the more convinced I am that I've seen your face somewhere."

Brady lit his cigarette, blew out a plume of smoke. "I wouldn't be surprised," he said calmly. "It was splashed all over the newspapers for long enough. I'm Matthew Brady."

There was a moment of absolute stillness and her eyes widened perceptibly. "Brady!" she said in a whisper. "But it isn't possible."

"Sorry to disappoint you, angel," he said. "But it is. I crashed-out of Manningham Gaol not much more than an hour ago."

She sat up, swinging her legs to the floor, and stubbed out her cigarette in the ash tray. "What do you want, Brady?" she said calmly, and she seemed to have recovered her nerve.

"I haven't got time to argue, so I'll give it to you

straight," Brady told her. "Jango tried to see me out of this world yesterday. With a little persuasion he told me that you'd put him up to it. I want to know why."

"I'll see you in hell first," she said. "Get out of here before I ring for the law."

She started to get up and Brady slapped her backhanded across the face, and pushed her back down on to the bed, a hand at her throat. "You'd better listen to me, you cheap tramp," he said. "If you put the cops on to me now or at any other time, I'll see that Jango pays. I've got friends inside—good friends. If I say the word, they'll make his face look like raw meat."

She glared up at him, but there was fear in her eyes —real fear and he knew that he had said the right thing. That Jango was important to her.

He took his hand away from her neck and she sat up, smoothing it with one hand. "What do you want to know?" she said sullenly.

"That's better," Brady said. "That's a whole lot better. Who asked you to sick Jango on to me?"

She took a cigarette from a box by the telephone and lit it from a table lighter. "It was a man called Das," she said. "He's an Indian—runs a phoney religious set-up called the Temple of Quiet about a mile from here, near the Hippodrome Theatre."

Brady frowned. "But I don't understand. I've never heard of him before."

She shrugged. "I'm telling you the truth. He's got his finger in everything crooked that goes on in these parts from drugs to girls. He came to see me on Wednesday. Told me he had a client who wanted to see you meet with a fatal accident inside. He said there was five hundred in it for us if Jango could handle it."

"And an extra two hundred and fifty if he managed it by today," Brady said.

She nodded. "That's right. If you want to know anything more, you'll have to see Das."

"I intend to," Brady said. He went to the door, unlocked it and turned. "Remember what I told you, Wilma. If I get nicked through you, Jango pays the piper."

She spat out one filthy, unprintable word at him and he gently closed the door and went along the corridor.

The girl in the cloakroom still looked bored. She gave him his coat and hat without a flicker of emotion and he put them on and went downstairs and out into the rain.

(5)

AS he walked away from the club the wind, blowing across the water, brought with it the dank, wet smell of rotting leaves, redolent with decay, filling him with a vague, irrational excitement.

The rain was falling in solid silver lances that gleamed in the lamplight as he went briskly towards the centre of the town through deserted streets. An occasional car swept by, and now and then, someone hurried along the sidewalk, head lowered against the driving rain.

He found an old man in tattered overcoat and cloth cap standing in a doorway on the corner of the main shopping street, hopefully trying to sell his last half-dozen Sunday newspapers. Brady bought one and the old man wiped a dewdrop from his nose with the back of a hand and stepped out into the rain to direct him.

He came to the Hippodrome first, a narrow,

marble-fronted Edwardian music hall with an alley running down one side to the stage door. The stills for that week's show were still on display in glass-fronted display cases and on impulse, he stopped and searched through them, looking for Anne Dunning.

He found several of her, mostly carefully posed in a tableau with two or three young male dancers, but there was one studio portrait which had really caught her. For a moment, he stayed there looking at it, remembering her kindness, and then he sighed and turned away.

The Temple of Quiet was up the next turning. There were many cars parked in the street and as he moved along the sidewalk, a large, black Mercedes swirled in to the kerb, splashing him with water from the gutter.

He turned angrily. "Why the hell don't you look where you're going?"

He caught a brief glimpse of a Homburg hat and pebble-dash glasses. Teeth gleamed whitely in the darkness. "So sorry," the man said with the merest suggestion of a lisp and drove the Mercedes farther along the street where there was more space.

Brady moved on to the gate of the temple and looked up at the imposing building with a frown. It looked as if it had been some kind of Nonconformist chapel at one time, a gaunt, soot-blackened Victorian building with fake Doric columns and a portico over the entrance. Probably the original congregation had dwindled away as the population tended to spread outwards from the centre of the city, and Das had got the place cheaply.

He mounted the broad steps into the portico,

opened one of the doors, and was immediately greeted by an overpowering smell of incense.

The hall was covered with an expensive Indian carpet and lit by fake electric tapers. A low hum of conversation came from somewhere in the dim recesses of the building and he followed the sound to a pair of double doors.

He stood outside listening for a while and then noticed another door at one side. He opened it and mounted a narrow stone staircase which brought him into a gallery from which he could see down into the hall below.

The altar and the choir stalls had been removed. In their place stood a gold-painted statue of Buddha. There were no chairs in the hall and the congregation sat cross-legged on the floor. They looked middle-aged and anxious and the majority were women.

The place was dimly lit with more fake tapers and heavy with incense. In front of the statue of Buddha, a small fire burned in a bowl and a man prayed before it, his head flat on the ground.

Brady decided that he must be Das. He looked very effective. He wore a yellow robe which left one shoulder bare and his head was shaved.

After a while he stood up and turned. He had a fine face and calm, wise eyes. He smiled gently and said in a melodious voice, "And so, my brethren, I give you a text to meditate upon until our next meeting. To do good is not enough. It is also necessary to *be* good."

He sounded completely sincere, but spoilt it for Brady in the next breath. "There will be the usual silver collection as you go out. Give what you can that we all may benefit."

He raised his arms in benediction and then turned and disappeared behind a screen.

The audience got to its feet, not without an effort in some cases, and Brady stayed where he was until the last of them had filed out.

He went downstairs and as he emerged into the corridor, a woman was about to enter a small office opposite. She wore a yellow robe rather similar to the one Das had been wearing and held a large collecting bag in one hand. It was bulging with cash.

"Can I help you?" she said with a slight frown.

She looked about forty and spinsterish, with one of those tight, desiccated faces and a slight nervous twitch to one side of her mouth.

"I'd like to see Mr. Das if that's possible," Brady told her.

"The Swami is always very tired after a service," she told him. "He doesn't usually see patients on a Sunday."

"It's most urgent," Brady assured her. She still appeared to be hesitating and he hastily took out two ten shilling notes and dropped them into the collecting bag. "The service was an inspiration."

"Wasn't it?" she said simply. "I'll see if the Swami can spare you a little time. Wait here, please."

She half-closed the office door, but Brady heard her pick up the telephone. There was a murmur of conversation and then she returned.

"The Swami is very tired, but he can spare you five minutes," she said. "Come this way, please."

A long, covered way connected the temple with what had once been the minister's house in the old days. When the woman opened the door at the far end, Brady was again conscious of that overpowering smell of incense.

They crossed a hall, the walls of which were hung with rich tapestries, and the woman knocked gently on a door and entered.

Brady moved in after her and stood there, hat in hand. The walls were draped in hand-embroidered Chinese dragon tapestries, and the floor was covered with a superb black carpet.

At one end of the room in an alcove, a small Buddha stood on an altar, incense burning in a bowl before it and Das knelt there, head bowed.

"Wait here until he is ready for you," the woman whispered and went out, quietly closing the door behind her.

In the centre of the room stood a beautiful hand-carved desk with a polished ebony top and round the walls on every side, was ranged a superb collection of Chinese pottery on specially constructed shelves.

Brady moved forward and examined a delicate porcelain vase. Behind him, there was a slight movement and Das said, "I see you are admiring my little collection. Are you an artist, by any chance?"

Brady shook his head. "You couldn't be more wrong. I'm an engineer, but I happen to admire anything that's beautifully constructed."

"Even a bridge can be a work of art," Das conceded. "If you are interested, the vase you were admiring is of the Ming Dynasty and worth well over a thousand pounds. It is the gem of my collection."

He caressed it lovingly with one slender hand then

moved across to the desk and sat down. He pointed to a chair opposite. "Mahroon tells me that you have a problem, my friend. That you require guidance."

"You could put it that way," Brady said, taking out a cigarette and lighting it. He sat down in the chair and dropped his hat to the floor. "My name's Matthew Brady. Does that mean anything to you?"

Das looked faintly surprised. "Should it do?"

"I should have thought so," Brady told him. "Considering the fact that you offered a fair price to see me dead this week."

Deep pain showed in the Hindu's fine liquid eyes. "I'm afraid I haven't the slightest idea of what you're talking about, Mr. Brady. Here we are concerned only with the conquest of self, we desire only to discover the truth which is to be found for each man in his own soul. The destruction of a fellow human being would be anathema to us."

"You can keep that kind of talk for the paying customers," Brady said.

Das sighed and pressed a buzzer on his desk. "I'm afraid I'll have to ask Mahroon to show you out."

"I should have thought you could have done rather better in the temple virgin line," Brady said. "She looks as if the sap's dried in her a long time ago. What was she when you roped her in—a schoolmistress?"

"You know you're really very insulting, Mr. Brady," Das said. "I'm afraid I'm going to have to do something about you. Something unpleasant."

There was a slight movement behind Brady, a brawny forearm slid round his neck, forcing back his chin, and he was jerked to his feet.

He was held as in a vice, unable even to turn round to see his assailant and Das leaned back in his chair and smiled. "I think the river, Mr. Brady. Yes, that will do very nicely. You slipped and fell crossing one of the wharves and the floodwaters carried you away. I'm really performing a public service."

"You'll never get away with it," Brady said desperately.

"Oh, but I will," Das assured him. "Sorry I can't hear how you managed to get out of Manningham, but we're rather short on time."

The chair was kicked out of the way and Brady was dragged backwards towards the door. He tried to struggle, but found himself helpless in that vice-like grip. In desperation he raised his right foot and ran it down the man's shin, crunching it into the instep with all his force.

His assailant gave a shriek of agony and released him. Brady turned quickly and looked up into the face of one of the biggest men he had ever seen in his life. Tiny pig-like eyes sparkled with rage in the flat, moronic face and a fist flailed out, catching Brady on the shoulder, sending him staggering across the room.

"Finish him, Shaun! Finish him!" Das cried, and Shaun lurched towards Brady, great broken-nailed hands swinging almost to his knees. Brady grabbed for a small lacquered table which stood near by and threw it at his legs, and Shaun tripped over it and fell to the floor.

Brady had no illusions about his chances in a fair fight. He moved in quickly, aiming a kick at Shaun's head, but there was nothing wrong with the big man's reflexes. He grabbed Brady's foot, twisted it, and brought him down.

They rolled wildly from side to side, limbs threshing, as Brady tried to pull free, but it was no use. Great hands wrapped themselves around his throat as Shaun rolled on top, and Brady started to choke.

The room suddenly seemed to go darker and Brady, struggling desperately, remembered an old Judo trick and spat in Shaun's face. The big man jerked his head back in a reflex action and Brady rammed his stiffened fingers into the bare throat just above the Adam's apple.

Shaun's mouth opened in a soundless scream and he fell backwards to roll on the floor in agony, hands tearing at his collar.

As Brady got to his feet, feeling his throat tenderly, Das moved round the desk on his way to the door. Brady got hold of the yellow robe, swung the Hindu round in a circle and pushed him back into his chair.

Das glared up at him. "You won't get away with this, Brady."

The fine face was twisted with rage and Brady grinned. "I wondered what you were really like under that phoney mask of yours. Now I know."

"I'll see you back inside if it's the last thing I do," Das said venomously.

"No you won't," Brady said. "If the law gets its paws on me again, I'll pull you down with me. I'll tell them you arranged my escape and turned nasty because I couldn't pay you what I'd promised."

"They'd never believe you," Das said contemptuously.

"I wouldn't be too sure about that. They've probably got a file on you a foot thick at least. I bet they're just waiting for you to make one false move."

"Get out of here!" Das screamed.

"Not until you've told me what I want to know," Brady said. "You asked Wilma Sutton to arrange for me to have a fatal accident, preferably by tonight. I'd like to know why."

"Go to hell!" Das said sullenly.

Brady shrugged and stood up. He walked across the room to the shelves on which the Hindu's collection was displayed, picked up a beautiful alabaster jar and hurled it at the wall.

It smashed into a score of pieces and Das jumped to his feet with a cry of dismay. "That's just to show you I mean business," Brady said. "My next trick's even better."

He picked up the Ming vase and raised it slowly above his head and Das cried out in horror. "For God's sake, no, Brady! I beg of you."

"Then start talking," Brady said. "I haven't got much time."

"A man came to see me last week," Das said hurriedly. "He was from London—a Hungarian called Anton Haras. He told me that it was necessary that you should die, that he was willing to pay well if I could arrange this."

"Who put him on to you?" Brady asked.

Das appeared to hesitate and Brady started to raise the vase again. "No, please, I'll tell you," the Hindu gabbled. "It was a contact of mine in London. We do business together from time to time."

"What name?"

"Soames—Professor Soames. He's a naturopath.

Has premises in Dell Street near Regent's Park. I've never met him. He's just a contact I use when I need certain merchandise."

Brady raised the vase in one quick movement and Das stumbled round the desk, arms outstretched. "I'm telling you the truth, I swear it."

For a moment Brady looked straight into the twisted, sweating face and then he handed the vase across. "You'd better be," he said.

Das clasped the vase to his chest with an audible sigh of relief and Brady walked across to the door, past Shaun who was sitting up now and moaning softly like some wounded animal, his face purple.

As Brady opened the door, Das said viciously, "Somebody wants you dead, Brady. I don't know why, I don't even know who. But I hope they get their hands on you before the police do."

Brady didn't bother to reply. He closed the door and moved back along the covered way to the temple. The woman was standing in the entrance hall in front of a small statue, head bowed in contemplation.

She turned as he approached and smiled. "Was the Swami able to help you?"

"I think you could say that," Brady told her.

"We, who have been shown the way, have much to thank him for."

"He's undoubtedly a most unusual man," Brady assured her solemnly and passed out into the night.

The door closed softly behind him and he paused for a moment on the top step. Obviously London was his next stop, but how was he going to get there? He had already spent half of the five pounds he had taken from the till at the shop, and the train fare would be more than that, he was sure.

Trying to hitch-hike would be fatal, but there was bound to be a transport café somewhere on the main road out of town. The sort of place where south-bound truck drivers stopped for a meal and a rest. If only he could get into the back of a truck without being seen, he could be in London for breakfast and no one the wiser.

The street was deserted except for one car parked a little higher up with its lights on. As he turned out through the main gate, the car started up and moved towards him.

It was the black Mercedes, the one which had splashed him with water earlier. He kept on walking at the same steady pace down towards the main road. Behind him there was a sudden burst of acceleration and the Mercedes bounced on to the pavement with the obvious intention of pinning him against the wall like a fly.

Brady jumped for the top of the railing and lifted his legs. Something seemed to pluck at his coat and then the Mercedes was back on the road and braking to a halt. As it started to reverse, he dropped to the pavement, turned and ran.

Tyres screamed behind him and a great finger of light picked him out of the darkness, throwing a gigantic shadow against a brick wall. He turned desperately and noticed a narrow opening to the left. He barely made it as the car skidded to a halt.

He was standing in the entrance to a narrow, stone-flagged footpath which ran between high stone walls and was lit, half-way along, by an old-fashioned gas lamp bracketed to one of the walls.

The car door slammed and Brady moved back into the shadows and waited. The man came forward and paused a few feet away, and the light from the gas lamp which illuminated the entrance to the footpath, glinted on the pebble-dash spectacles beneath the Homburg hat.

The collar of his heavy, Continental greatcoat was turned up to obscure his face, but his teeth showed in a pleasant smile and he said in his peculiar lisping voice, "Let's be sensible about this, Brady."

"Suits me," Brady said. "Who the hell are you? Anton Haras?"

The man laughed once, coldly, and raised his right hand. Brady ducked as flame stabbed through the night. There was a muffled cough and a bullet ricocheted from the wall behind him.

Once, sitting in a café in Havana before the Castro regime, he had seen a man assassinated at the next table. The killer had used a Mauser with an SS bulbous silencer and it had made just such a noise. Brady turned and ran, his eyes fixed on the gas lamp halfway along the footpath.

Feet pounded over the flagstones behind him, the sound echoing from the walls and again, there came that peculiar muffled cough and something whispered past his ear.

He stumbled to his knees and his fingers fastened over a large stone. As he scrambled up, he hurled it at the gas lamp, plunging the footpath into darkness, and ran on.

He came out into the narrow alley at the side of the

Hippodrome Theatre at a dead run. A few yards down on the left-hand side was the stage door, a small lamp still turned on above it.

As Brady ran forward, the door opened and a woman emerged. She carried a small grip in one hand and turned to lock the door. Brady slipped on the greasy cobbles and stumbled against an overflowing dustbin, the lid falling to the ground with a clatter.

She turned in alarm and he looked down into the white, frightened face of Anne Dunning.

"Don't be afraid," he gasped.

The scream died in her throat and she gazed up at him wide-eyed. "But I don't understand, Mr. Brady. Have they released you?"

The Mauser coughed again and the lamp above the door shattered. Brady caught a fleeting glimpse of Haras standing in the entrance to the footpath.

He kicked the door open and pushed Anne Dunning inside and along the corridor. "No time to explain," he said. "There's a man out there with a gun and he's doing his level best to kill me."

As they turned the corner at the end of the corridor, the door burst open and Haras came after them.

Brady paused, one hand gripping the girl's arm. "What's down here?"

"Dressing-rooms," she said.

He pulled her up a flight of stairs to the left and they came out in to the wings at one side of the stage. Haras followed them, running surprisingly well for a man of his weight. A single light illuminated the stage and Brady and the girl went across to the temporary safety of the shadows on the other side.

Brady made to go down a short flight of steps, but

she pulled him back. "No good, that door's locked. In here!"

There was another door almost hidden behind some scenery flats and she opened it quickly and dragged him inside. She shot the bolt and they stood there in the darkness and waited.

Haras ran into the wings and paused. After a moment, he went down the steps and tried the door, shaking the handle angrily, and then he returned and went back on stage.

"I'd give a lot to have a gun in my hand right now," Brady said softly.

The girl clicked on the light. The room was crowded with old costumes and scenery, even furniture, the accumulation of the years.

She moved across to a cupboard, opened it, and turned with a .38 calibre revolver in her hand. "Will this do? It's only a stage prop, I'm afraid. We used it in the play. There's a box of blanks here, though."

Brady broke open the chamber and examined it, sudden, nervous excitement stirring inside him. "I might be able to scare the bastard off, if nothing else."

She opened the box of cartridges and he quickly loaded the weapon, then crossed to the door and pulled back the bolt.

She moved to his shoulder as he turned off the light and he was aware of the warmth, of the fragrance of her, so near to him in the darkness.

"You keep well back," he ordered. "This is my affair. I don't want you to get hurt."

He opened the door gently and looked out. Haras was standing in the centre of the stage, staring out into the auditorium.

"It's no use running, Brady," he called. "You can't get away."

"Haras!" Brady said softly.

As the Hungarian turned, Brady raised the revolver and fired and the report seemed deafening. Haras disappeared with surprising speed into the shadows opposite.

Brady crouched down and Anne Dunning moved beside him. "Where's the switch that operates the stage light?" he asked softly.

"Right behind us. Shall I turn it off?"

He nodded and a moment later, the theatre was plunged into darkness.

"I'm coming to get you, Haras!" Brady shouted.

A tongue of flame answered him from the darkness. He fired twice in reply and moved across the stage, crouching. Haras went down the stairs ahead of him and ran along the corridor. As Brady turned the corner, the stage door banged.

It was quiet and somehow peaceful out in the alley with the rain hissing down. Brady stood at the end of the footpath and listened to the echo of the Hungarian's running feet. Faintly from the distance, a car door closed hollowly. A moment later an engine started up.

"That old gun did the trick with a vengeance," Anne Dunning said from behind and her voice was breathless and excited.

As he turned to answer her, a strange, unearthly wailing sounded far away in the darkness, echoing through the night in a dying fall.

He shivered, standing there with the rain falling on him, and a wave of greyness ran through him. The girl looked up, a strange expression on her face. "What is it?"

"The general alarm at Manningham Gaol," he said simply. "It means that from now on, they'll be looking for me."

(6)

THEY went back into the theatre and she turned on the lights and sat on a wooden chair, chin cupped in one hand, while Brady told her everything.

When he had finished, she sighed and shook her head in bewilderment. "The whole affair sounds like some horrible nightmare, except for one thing."

"Haras?" Brady said.

She nodded soberly. "Yes, he makes it all so frighteningly real. The thing is, what do you do now?"

"Try to get to London. It's all I *can* do. After all, this Professor Soames character is my only lead."

"Won't that be difficult now they know you're out?"

He nodded grimly. "You can say that again. I was hoping they wouldn't miss me till breakfast, but something must have gone wrong. I could have been in London with a breathing space to do my checking while they still looked for me in Manningham."

"The question is, how will you get there?"

"The sixty-four-thousand dollar question with a vengeance," he told her.

She appeared to be thinking hard. After a while, she said, "Did you know my father was a prisoner in Germany during the last war?"

Brady nodded. "He did mention something about it once."

"He got out three times," she said. "Finally, he made it right through Germany and France and over the Pyrenees into Spain. He said the important things to remember were to keep off the roads and to get where you wanted to be in the fastest possible way."

"It's a nice theory," Brady said. "In practice it might be a little more difficult. There's the night express to London, but I've about as much chance of getting on that now as I'd have of breaking into Fort Knox."

"I'm going to London tonight myself," she said. "I've booked a sleeper. The others went this morning, but I wanted to see some friends before I left. They live about twelve miles out of town. I've spent the day with them."

"The show folded then?"

"I'm afraid it fell flat on its face." She frowned suddenly. "Wait a minute. I've just had an idea. That's a single sleeper I've booked. I hate sharing with a stranger, so I paid the extra. If we could get you on board somehow, you could travel to London in comfort with me."

"It wouldn't be possible," he said. "The station will be crawling with police. They're bound to watch the trains. I'd never get through the barrier."

"My father once walked out through the main gates

of a German prison camp. He looked so familiar, they didn't even question him."

He frowned. "I don't understand."

"He was wearing a German uniform."

"And how does that help me?"

"But it's so simple," she explained. "Who on earth would think twice about a porter carrying a lady's luggage to the train? He takes it to her compartment and stays there. It's as simple as that."

"There's the small matter of a uniform to start with," he said.

She laughed gaily and got to her feet. "You're forgetting you're in a theatre."

He followed her into the wings and she opened the door of the props room, switched on the light and started to rummage in a large, wicker basket.

After a moment or two, she turned triumphantly and tossed a peaked cap across to him. "That'll do for a start."

The white metal badge said British Railways and Brady tried the cap on and examined himself in the mirror. It was a couple of sizes too large, which was an advantage, and she came and stood behind him, a dark serge suit with shiny official buttons on it, hanging over her arm.

"The problem's solved," she said, her face gay and animated. For a moment, she looked like a young child involved in some new and exciting game.

Brady turned, his face serious. "It's no good," he told her. "It means involving you up to your pretty neck and I can't have that. They're pretty rough on people who help escaped convicts on the run. You catch that train as you planned. I'll find some other way of getting to London."

"I'm involved in this business whether you like it or not," she said forcefully. "My father thought a lot of you. When I visited you the other day, I could see why, because beneath the anger and the bitterness and the frustration, there was still something of the real Matthew Brady."

"But you'll only end up getting hurt," he protested.

"Let's put it this way," she said patiently. "I'm going to help you whether you damned well like it or not."

He looked at her with something like wonder in his eyes and shook his head. "You're more of your father's daughter than I thought."

She smiled, conscious that she had won. "Let's get out of here. My digs are just around the corner. We can stay there till train time."

"What about your landlady?"

"No trouble there. She's spending the night with her sister. Told me to leave the key under the mat when I left."

She found a piece of brown paper in which to wrap the uniform and they left, locking the stage door behind them. It was still raining heavily and they went along the alley and turned boldly into the main street.

She took his arm and they walked at a steady unhurried pace, past the lighted windows of the shops, turning into a side street as a police car rounded the corner, skidding slightly on the wet road.

It roared away into the night, bell ringing shrilly and Brady grinned tightly. "They'll turn this town upside down before they're through."

"You'll be on your way to London before they get properly started," she said calmly.

The street was lined with old, brownstone Victorian terrace houses, each with a narrow strip of garden running down to the road. She opened the gate to one of them, and as he followed her along the path, Brady shook his head in bewilderment. There was something elusive about her, a quality he couldn't quite pin down, that made her different from any other woman he'd ever known. Nothing seemed to disturb her composure.

She opened the front door, led the way along the hall, and moved into a large, comfortable living-room. She switched on a large electric fire and turned with a smile. "I'll see to my packing first, then I'll make some coffee. You take it easy and have a smoke. You look as if you could sleep for a day at least."

After she had gone, he lit a cigarette and sat in front of the electric fire and tried to relax. He found it quite impossible. The rain tapped insistently against the window as if trying to get in, and his stomach was suddenly hollow with nervous excitement. For the moment, he was safe and warm, but once outside the door, he was a hunted man with every hand raised against him.

He shivered slightly, feeling suddenly afraid. As he stood up, he noticed an old upright piano against the far wall. He opened the lid and played a few chords. The keys were yellow with age, but it was in tune and he sat down and slipped into an old Rodgers and Hart number. Nostalgic and wistful, a hint of a summer which was gone and memories only now.

He passed from one number easily into another, concentrating on his playing so that the fear left him, and after a while, he glanced up and saw that Anne Dunning was standing at his side.

"You play very well, Mr Brady," she said.

"One of my few accomplishments." He grinned. "And the name's Matt."

She smiled, her eyes crinkling slightly at the corners. "I'll make that coffee now—Matt. You can change into your uniform while you're waiting. I've laid it out for you on the bed. First room on your right at the top of the stairs."

The room was as old-fashioned as the rest of the house with a great brass-railed bed and heavy Victorian furniture. Two suitcases stood on the floor by the door, another lay on the bed beside the uniform, open and empty. She had obviously rearranged her packing to make room for his tweed suit and trench-coat.

He changed quickly and stood in front of the long mirror of the wardrobe and examined himself. A stranger stared out at him. The uniform itself was a size too small and tight under the armpits, but the cap pulled well down over his eyes, the peak shading his face, made all the difference. He folded his suit and trench-coat neatly, packed them in the empty suitcase and carried it downstairs with the others.

Anne was still in the kitchen and he went and leaned in the doorway. After a moment, she turned to reach for something and saw him. She gave an involuntary gasp and stepped back and then she burst into laughter. "But that's wonderful, Matt. It just isn't you any longer."

He pushed the cap to the back of his head and grinned. "Well, that's taken a load off my mind. When do we start?"

She carried a loaded tray into the living-room and he followed her. "The train leaves just after midnight. We can board any time after eleven. I think it would be as well to make it as close to midnight as possible."

He nodded in agreement as she handed him a cup of coffee. "That makes sense. How long will it take us to get to the station?

She shrugged. "About ten minutes, a little longer if we keep to the back streets. We come out at the side of a large hotel and the station's on the opposite side of a square."

"That sounds good," he said. "Anyone seeing us crossing the square will assume I'm bringing your bags across from the hotel."

She nodded. "That's what I thought."

They had another cup of coffee each and after a while, she took the tray back to the kitchen. Brady lit another cigarette, lay back in the chair and tried to relax.

Ten minutes later, she came in wearing her rain-coat and a dark beret. He got to his feet and grinned. "Ready to roll?"

She nodded. "How do you feel?"

"Completely numb," he said. "But I'll survive."

They left by the back door, moving out through a small, dark yard into a narrow alley at the rear. The rain had slackened a little and she crossed from one street into another as if she knew exactly where she was going.

They met no one and in little more than fifteen

minutes from leaving the house, moved along the narrow street which entered into the main square.

Brady was conscious of the weight of the three suitcases. He paused by the side entrance of the hotel to get a firmer grip on them, and then started across the cobbled square after Anne.

She walked ahead, calm and unhurried, completely sure of herself. There were three police cars parked outside the main entrance to the station. She glanced at them casually and went straight up the steps and into the hall without hesitating.

It was cold and cheerless, the kiosks all closed for the night, but the station restaurant was still open and there were a surprising number of people scattered round the great arched hall waiting for trains.

Two uniformed police constables stood by the ticket barrier, scrutinizing carefully everyone who passed through. Anne had her ticket ready. There was the briefest of pauses while the ticket collector inspected it, and then she was through, Brady trailing at her heels with the suitcases.

The train stood waiting at the platform, a wisp of steam drifting gently up between the wheels of the engine. The sleepers were at the far end and Brady's hands were moist with sweat, his mouth dry.

The young policeman who stood by the entrance to the coach was tired. His mouth opened in a yawn and he raised one hand to stifle it as Anne moved past him.

She handed her ticket to the attendant who stood waiting in his tiny cubicle and he checked it quickly with his register. "The first compartment in the next coach, Miss Dunning. Number twelve. Would you like tea in the morning?

She shook her head. "I'll breakfast later, somewhere in town."

He returned her ticket and smiled. "We get into King's Cross at seven, but you don't need to leave the train until eight."

As another passenger came through the entrance, Anne moved away along the corridor and Brady followed her. They passed through into the next coach. It was quiet and deserted and she quickly opened the door of the compartment and led the way in.

Brady dropped the suitcases, removed his cap and leaned against the door. His forehead was damp with sweat and he whistled softly.

"I wouldn't like to have to go through that lot again."

Her eyes were shining with excitement and she flung her arms around his neck and hugged him. "I told you it would work."

He held her close for a moment, conscious of her warm body, young and vital and alive and after a moment, she gently disengaged herself. "We'd better start making plans," she said lightly and took off her raincoat.

The compartment was narrow and cramped, with a single bunk against one wall and a washbasin in the corner by the window. Brady sat on the edge of the bunk and lit a cigarette. "What do I do if anyone knocks on the door?"

She glanced round the compartment and smiled. "Get under the bunk, I suppose. There doesn't seem to be much choice."

"And what happens when we reach King's Cross?"

She shrugged. "Once through the barrier, straight down into the Underground. I've got a flat in Kensington. We can be there in twenty minutes. Actually I share it with another girl, but she's doing a show in Glasgow this week."

"What about my uniform?"

"That's simple," she said. "As we go through the barrier, I'll carry my coat over my arm with yours hidden underneath. You can slip it on when we get down into the Underground. It's always crowded with people at that time in the morning. You could stand on your head and nobody would notice."

Brady grinned. "You've got it all organized, haven't you?"

"Somebody's got to think of these things."

As she talked, she unzipped her dress and pulled it over her head. She stood there in her slip with a complete lack of self-consciousness and opened one of the suitcases. She took out a red silk brocade housecoat and put it on.

As she fastened it at the waist, she smiled. "That'll have to do me for tonight." Brady nodded and suddenly his head seemed too heavy for his body. He took a deep breath and made an effort to sit up straight and she knelt down and started to untie his shoes. "You need some sleep, and badly," she said.

Brady unfastened his collar at the neck and took off the jacket. She pulled off his shoes and pushed him back down on to the bunk.

"What about you?" he protested.

"There's room for both of us," she said and lay down

on the bunk beside him and spread a blanket over them.

Brady was too tired to argue. He turned and looked at her dark head lying there on the pillow beside him and grinned. "You're a funny girl," he said softly.

She smiled and it was as if a light had turned on inside her and a radiance glowed out of the dark eyes. No woman had ever smiled at him quite like that before, drawing him in, enveloping him.

He leaned forward and kissed her once, very gently upon her parted mouth and she turned her face into his shoulder and after a while, they slept.

It was the knock on the door which awakened him, bringing him back to life from a deep, dreamless sleep. Anne was pulling her dress over her head and she turned quickly and nodded reassuringly. "Only the attendant knocking people up," she said.

"Are we there?" Brady said in surprise.

She nodded and he swung his legs to the floor and pulled on his shoes. He felt completely refreshed and relaxed, but his stomach was hollow and empty and he realized, with a sense of shock, that he hadn't eaten since leaving the gaol.

They dressed quickly and when they were ready, she opened the door and peered cautiously out into the corridor. She turned and nodded and Brady picked up the cases and moved past her.

As he went along the corridor, a door opened and a man emerged from a compartment carrying a small overnight bag. Brady paused to let him go first and then followed close behind.

There were no uniformed policemen standing at the barrier, but Brady noticed two large men in raincoats and soft hats leaning against the wall by the newspaper stand and they seemed to be examining faces as people moved out through the gate.

A yard or two in front of Brady, a porter drove a small electric truck loaded with sacks of mail and as he approached the barrier, someone opened the vehicle gate for him. Brady didn't hesitate. He followed the truck through, nodded his thanks to the man on the gate, and moved straight across the hall towards the entrance to the Underground.

He joined the descending stream of people and after a while, was conscious of Anne at his shoulder. When they reached the hall below, he put down the suitcases in a corner and she handed him his trench-coat.

"I'll get the tickets," she said and moved across to the machines.

The hall was crowded with people and Brady quickly pulled on the coat and belted it around his waist. Then, quite casually, he took off the cap and pulled the rain hat from his pocket.

He pulled it into shape and put it on as Anne returned. "All set?" she said.

He crushed the porter's cap between his hands and thrust it into his pocket. "All set," he replied, and picking up the cases, followed her to the barrier.

(7)

HER flat was on the third floor of an old, grey stone house overlooking a quiet square near Kensington Gardens. When she opened the door, the curtains were drawn and the room was in half-darkness.

She pulled them back and opened the window. "The place needs a good airing," she said. "It hasn't been lived in for three or four weeks."

Brady put down the suitcases and closed the door. "It looks pretty good to me," he said, taking off his trench-coat.

"How hungry are you?" she demanded.

He grinned. "Believe it or not, I last ate as a guest of Her Majesty."

Her eyes widened perceptibly. "You must be starving. Why didn't you mention food when we were at my digs in Manningham?"

He shrugged. "There seemed to be rather more important things to worry about."

She smiled. "Never mind, there's a little shop just round the corner. I'll run down and see what they've got. You make yourself comfortable. I shan't be long."

When she had gone, he explored the small flat. There was the large living-room, a kitchen, one bedroom with twin beds and the bathroom. He turned on both taps and started to undress.

He was wallowing up to his chin in hot water, the room half-full of steam, when the door opened a fraction and a hand reached in to deposit a small package on one of the glass shelves.

"Breakfast in fifteen minutes," she called and the door closed again.

The package contained a cheap razor, a packet of blades and a tube of shaving cream. He smiled to himself and quickly lathered his face. When he left the bathroom ten minutes later, freshly shaved, his hair combed, wearing the tweed suit, he felt civilized for the first time in months.

The table was laid for two in the bow window and a newspaper was propped against the sugar-bowl. He sat down and picked it up eagerly.

He was on the front page, down in the right-hand corner. The prison authorities hadn't issued details as to how he had escaped. There was a brief account of the circumstances of his trial, a warning that he was dangerous, and an interview with the Chief Constable of Manningham who was quite certain he was still in the town and anticipated an early arrest.

The photograph had been taken from his record card and he examined it with a slight frown, wondering whether there could be any connexion between himself and this gaunt stranger.

"It doesn't look much like you," Anne said at his shoulder.

"It's perhaps as well," he told her. "They're not going to look for me in Manningham indefinitely."

She placed ham and eggs before him and a plate piled high with toast. "I'm strictly limited in the kitchen at the best of times," she said, sitting down opposite him. "I hope that suits your transatlantic palate."

He grinned. "Absolutely no complaints. I haven't felt so hungry since I was a boy, coming in from fishing in the bay in the early morning."

"Where was that?" she said.

"Near Cape Cod," he told her. "My father had a farm right on the coast."

"I've always wanted to visit the New England states," she said.

"Until you've seen our fall, you haven't lived," he told her. "There's nothing like it on God's earth."

They lit cigarettes and he gazed out of the window through the light rain down into the trees in the square, watching their leaves twist and fall in the slight breeze, thinking of home.

"Would you like to go back some day?" she said softly.

He nodded. "Funnily enough, I was going to go home after the Kuwait job. I'd had a letter from my brother-in-law. He's an architect, senior partner in a large Boston firm. He wanted me to join them."

"Perhaps you will when you get this thing sorted out."

He turned and smiled. "Maybe you're right, but sitting here on my backside isn't going to help. I'd better get started."

"Don't be a fool." She laid a restraining hand on his arm. "You can't go walking round London for long and expect to get away with it. Sooner or later, you'll turn a corner and walk right into the arms of some young constable, pounding his beat and just dying for quick promotion. What would that prove?"

"What do you suggest?" he demanded impatiently.

"I'll hire a car for the day. It won't cost much and there's a garage just round the corner. You'll be a lot safer driving round London than walking."

He took hold of one of her hands. "I'm beginning to wonder where I'd be without you."

She flushed and stood up, with a slight smile. "Flattery will get you nowhere. If you want to work for your keep, you can clear the table while I go and see about the car."

The door closed behind her and he sat there for a while, finishing his cigarette and thinking about her. He stood by the window and watched her go down the steps and walk along the sidewalk and suddenly, there was a hollow ache in his stomach and he knew that she had become important to him.

He cleared the table and had just finished washing-up when she returned. "That was quick," he said.

She smiled. "Oh, they know me. I've done this several times since I've been living here. I've checked up on Dell Street, by the way. It's near Regent's Park. Allowing for the traffic, it shouldn't take us more than twenty minutes to get there."

He frowned and gripped her arms tightly. "There's

no need for you to come. I don't even know what I might be running into."

"The car's in my name," she said calmly. "And according to the insurance, no one else is supposed to drive. I'm in this up to my neck now, Matt. You'll just have to get used to the idea."

He sighed. "Okay, Anne. You win. Let's get going."

The car was a small Morris saloon, just the thing for the heavy London traffic and she handled it expertly, nosing her way into the main traffic stream of the Bayswater Road and turning into Marylebone Road towards Regent's Park.

They found Dell Street with little difficulty, a quiet backwater near the park, tall Victorian town houses in their own grounds.

Professor Soames's premises were certainly imposing and the flat-roofed extensions at the rear of the house looked as if they had only been recently completed.

The large double gates stood open and Anne drove past and parked the car in a small cul-de-sac a few yards along the street.

Brady looked out through the rear window to the gold-painted board fastened to the wall by the gate. It said *Deepdene Nursing Home* and underneath *Professor H. Soames—Naturopath.*

"Quite a set-up," he said.

Anne nodded and switched off the engine. "What now?"

He shrugged. "I'll just walk in and ask to see him. Pretend to be a prospective patient. It's the only way to handle it."

"And then?"

Brady grinned. "I think he'll see reason. If he's running a place like this, scandal's the last thing he'll want."

She shook her head decidedly. "It's no good. Perhaps he isn't available today. He may even be out of town."

"Then what do you suggest?"

She shrugged. "It's obvious. I go in first and ask for an appointment. If he's available, then there's no harm done. If he isn't, we can come back later." He opened his mouth to argue and she stopped it gently with one hand. "The less people see of your face, the better."

She got out of the car and closed the door. As she started to move away, she paused and took the car keys from her purse. "Here, you'd better have these," she said. "Just in case you have to move in a hurry."

After she had gone, Brady lit a cigarette and settled back in his seat to wait. She was quite right, of course. There was no sense in his simply walking in, taking the risk that someone might recognize him and all to no purpose. Certainly there could be no danger for the girl in simply asking for an appointment. At least he would know whether Soames was available or not.

There was an old newspaper in the glove compartment and he worked his way through it systematically, killing time as he waited.

He only really started to feel uneasy when an hour had gone by. He lit another cigarette and looked back through the rear window at the gate, but there was no sign of her and he cursed and turned back to check the clock on the dashboard.

Which ever way he looked at it, something had obviously gone wrong. He gave her another twenty minutes and then got out of the car, locked the door and slipped the keys into the ticket pocket of his pants.

The street was quiet and deserted as he crossed to the gates and entered. There was still a fine drizzle falling and he followed the broad sweep of the gravel drive and mounted the steps to the front door.

It opened to his touch and he passed through into a pleasant, carpeted hall. A low, contemporary desk stood in one corner and a young woman was absorbed in sorting a card index.

She was extremely attractive, with red-gold hair swinging shoulder-length, and wore a white medical smock which gaped at the neck as she bent over, revealing the deep valley between her breasts.

She glanced up and smiled professionally. "Yes, sir?"

"I wonder if I might see Professor Soames?" he said.

"I'm afraid the professor only sees patients by appointment, sir."

"I realize that," Brady told her. "But a friend of mine recommended me to try him. I've had a history of back trouble and severe pain for several years now since an old injury."

"I'm afraid the professor is booked-up for today," she said. "However, we do have several other perfectly competent naturopaths on our staff."

"It must be the professor," Brady said emphatically. "He's the only one who can help me. I'm convinced of that after what my friend told me."

She sighed and made a note on a pad. "If you'll give me your name, sir. I'll see what I can do."

"Harlow," Brady said. "George Harlow."

She wrote it down and then swivelled in her chair, uncrossing her silk-clad legs, and got to her feet in one fluid movement. "Please take a seat, Mr. Harlow. I shan't be a moment."

She walked across the hall with an easy, confident grace and opened a door. As it closed, Brady grinned and sat on the edge of the desk. If she was a sample of the staff, this must be quite a place.

There was an appointment register lying open beside the card index and he turned it round quickly and ran a finger down the page. There was no sign of an appointment in Anne's name and he frowned and turned the register round again.

"Will you come this way, Mr. Harlow? I think we can fit you in."

The girl had approached soundlessly, her footsteps deadened by the thick carpet. She gave no sign that she had seen him examining the register and yet she must have done.

Brady smiled. "It's very kind of you to go to so much trouble."

She led the way along a narrow corridor which led into the extension at the rear and opened a door. Brady walked in and found himself in a small, comfortably furnished dressing-room.

"Someone will be with you in just a moment, Mr. Harlow. Perhaps you'd like to get undressed. You'll find a bathrobe behind the door."

"Undressed?" Brady said. "Is that really necessary?"

"Professor Soames prefers patients to be completely

relaxed before an examination," she explained. "You'll spend a little time in the steam room and have a relaxing massage. The professor will see you afterwards."

The door closed behind her and Brady shrugged and took off his coat. If this was the only way open to him of getting to see Soames then he had no choice.

He wrapped a towel about his waist and put on the bathrobe and waited. A few minutes later, the door opened and another young woman wearing a white medical smock tightly belted at the waist, came in.

She was, if anything, even more attractive than the receptionist. The smock was damp with moisture and clung to her figure, moulding each curve.

She pushed a tendril of dark hair back from her forehead and smiled. "Mr. Harlow, will you come this way, please?"

As he followed her along the corridor, Brady wondered just how relaxed the professor expected his patients to be. The girl opened a swing door and they passed straight into a long tiled room, thick with steam.

A squat, obese old gentleman with a towel about his waist, passed them, another attractive young woman in white smock assisting him. Each side of the room was lined with cubicles, the interiors masked by plastic curtains.

An atmosphere of brooding quiet hung over the place and then a woman laughed as they passed one of the cubicles. Brady turned his head quickly and noticed that the curtain wasn't properly drawn.

Another fat and aging gentleman lay face down on

a couch while a young woman massaged him. She wasn't wearing her white smock. In fact she wasn't wearing anything.

Things were becoming a little clearer. At least it was possible to understand how Soames could have a connexion with a man like Das.

The girl went through another swing door and they entered a quiet white-tiled corridor. There was a door at the end marked private and she opened it and Brady followed her in.

This room was also white-tiled and heavy with steam. There was a shower stall in one corner and a large padded table in the centre.

The man who stood beside it wore only bathing shorts and his body was strong and powerful, muscles standing out like great knots. The face was heavy-boned and hard, eyes cold, hair close-cropped to the skull.

"This is Mr. Harlow, Karl," the girl said. "Will you get him ready? The professor will be along in ten minutes."

Karl's English was good, but with a heavy German accent. "You will please take off your bathrobe," he said politely.

Brady obliged and the German led him across to the shower stall and pushed him inside. The heavy glass door closed and a score of needle jets came to life and played upon his body forcefully.

It was not only that the water was ice-cold, the jets themselves were physically painful. He stuck it for two or three minutes and then tried to open the door.

It was locked. He hammered on the glass and Karl frowned his surprise, pointed to his watch and shook his head. The German turned a valve and the jets increased in force until Brady was crouched down on the floor, gasping with breath, fighting against the agony.

When the door opened, he fell on to the floor and the German lifted him and grinned, exposing bad teeth. "How do you feel now, Mr. Harlow?"

"More dead than alive," Brady gasped. "Is that supposed to do me good?"

The German grinned again. "Oh, no, Mr. Brady. It's supposed to soften you up."

Brady was not really conscious of the blow itself, simply of something exploding in the pit of his stomach and then the white tiles lifted to meet him.

He was not unconscious because he could hear voices far away in the distance as the pain swelled in his body to a peak of agony and then retreated like the tide. Slowly the blackness turned to grey and then he was aware of the light directly above his head, set in the ceiling like some baleful eye, its rays diffused by the steam.

There was no longer pain, only a warmth spreading throughout his body as expert hands massaged his stomach muscles. He groaned and tried to get up. A hand pushed him back down and a harsh American voice said, "Take it easy, lover. You're doing fine."

He closed his eyes, breathed deeply for a moment or two, opened them again.

A woman leaned over him, but such a woman as he had never seen before. Long black hair framed a man's face, hard and big-boned with a wide, fleshy mouth.

She was well over six feet in height and the sleeves of her white smock were rolled back to expose biceps a wrestler might have envied.

"Who the hell are you?" Brady said.

"Soames," she said calmly. "I guess you got my sex wrong, lover."

Brady sat up and rubbed his stomach. "I suppose Das telephoned you from Manningham?"

She nodded. "I never thought you'd make it, not with the dragnet the cops have got out for you. You must be quite a man, lover."

Brady hesitated for a moment. "There was a girl. She tried to see you earlier. What happened to her?"

Soames grinned. "I thought there was a connexion. She got my sex wrong, too. Said she'd been recommended to see me by a satisfied patient. It just didn't jell. I only handle men."

"I bet you do," Brady said. "Is the girl all right?"

She nodded. "For the time being."

Her words carried an implied threat, but there was little he could do about it at the moment. He tightened the towel at his waist and stood up. "What now?"

She opened the door and the German stepped into the room. "Karl will take you to get dressed. When you're ready, he'll bring you to my private office for a chat." She paused in the doorway. "Don't try to make a run for it, lover. I wouldn't want to have you roughed up again. It isn't often I get the chance of having a chat with someone from the old country."

When she had gone, Brady turned to the German and raised his right fist. "Any time you feel like trying again, just say the word."

Karl tossed Brady's bathrobe into his face. "Put that on, and hurry."

He was wearing a tee shirt, white jacket and pants. Brady grinned. "You look real pretty, Karl. I bet the old boys go for you in a big way."

The German's face became suffused with passion. He pulled Brady close, produced a .38 revolver with a specially shortened barrel from his pocket, and tapped him in the face. "Now or later, Brady. It makes no difference to me. If you want a few more hours, keep your mouth shut."

He pushed Brady out into the corridor and through the main steam room past the cubicles. Brady took his time over getting dressed, his mind racing. Unless the German had been trying to frighten him, there was only going to be one end to this business.

He was more worried about Anne than he was about himself. As they mounted the back stairs, he thought of her alone in this place, helpless, perhaps in Karl's tender care.

The thought filled him with sudden quick rage and he hesitated, but the German prodded him in the back with the .38. "Keep moving!" he grated.

Soames was waiting in her office at the end of the corridor. It was beautifully furnished in contemporary style, the walls decorated in pastel shades of blue and hand-made silk wallpaper.

The desk was a sheet of black glass and she sat on the other side, a cigarette in a long, silver holder jutting out of the side of her mouth, and signing letters.

She looked up at him calmly. "You look fine, lover. Just fine. Karl, wait outside in the corridor."

The German went without a murmur and she

grinned again. "A good boy, Karl. A trifle psychopathic at times, but the clients love him."

"You've got quite a place here," Brady said.

She shrugged. "I give the public what it wants. My girls are all trained masseurs with diplomas to prove it. Nobody can lay a finger on me."

There was coffee on a side table and she filled two cups. "Cream and sugar?"

"Both," Brady said.

She pushed a cup across to him. "Which part of the States do you hail from?"

He told her and drank some of his coffee. It was good—very good. He swallowed the rest and put the delicate cup down carefully. "Let's cut the polite conversation and get down to business. Why do you want to see me dead?"

She put down her cup and lit another cigarette. "But I don't. Not even a little bit."

"Then what about Haras?" Brady said. "You put him in touch with Das, didn't you?"

She shook her head and said tranquilly, "I never heard of Haras until Das spoke to me on the phone. It was someone else who asked me if I had a reliable contact in Manningham. An old friend."

"Then Haras must be tied in with this other person?"

"That's right, lover."

"And you've no intention of giving me the name?"

"For the moment, not a chance. I've been in touch and she's asked me to hold you for the time being. You'll have to take it easy and await developments."

"So it's another woman?"

"That's right, lover. Surprised?"

"Nothing could surprise me any more." His head was aching and her eyes seemed suddenly enormous like black holes in her white face. He said slowly, "What about Anne?"

"Your girl friend?" She shrugged. "Don't worry about her. I've got a friend in Port Said who can always use fresh talent."

A cold nausea seeped through him. "You'll never get away with it," he said.

She sounded genuinely surprised. "Oh, but I will. It's surprising how quickly even the most stubborn girls will come to heel—especially when the right methods are applied."

"You lousy bitch!" he said, but his voice seemed to belong to someone else.

He tried to get up, but all the strength had drained from his body.

She smiled. "Just go with the tide, lover. Have a nice, long sleep."

Her voice seemed to come from the other side of the hill and he slumped forward across the desk.

(8)

HE drifted up from a deep well of darkness and agony exploded inside his head as a hand slapped him heavily across the face. He felt no pain—no pain at all. It was as if his body no longer belonged to him. Each sound seemed to come from far away across water and yet he could hear everything with the most extraordinary clarity.

"How is he?" Soames asked.

Karl laughed harshly. "Good for another couple of hours at least."

"I should know what they want doing with him by then," Soames replied.

Their voices faded and the door closed. Brady opened his eyes slowly. The room was festooned with cobwebs—giant grey cobwebs that stretched from one wall to another and undulated slowly.

He closed his eyes and breathed deeply, fighting the

panic which rose inside him. When he opened them again, the cobwebs had almost disappeared.

He was lying on a narrow, single bed against one wall of a small room. A shaded light hung down from the ceiling and curtains were drawn across the window.

He swung his legs down to the floor and sat on the edge of the bed for a while before trying to stand. There was a bad taste in his mouth and his tongue was dry and swollen. Whatever had gone into that coffee had been good—very good.

He got to his feet and lurched across the room, steadied himself against the opposite wall, then turned and moved back to the bed. After a while, the cobwebs disappeared completely and suddenly and everything clicked back into normality.

The door was securely locked and there was no transom. He sat on the edge of the bed and considered the situation. He didn't have a great deal of time to spare.

By now, the police search had probably extended to London. He had to get out of here. And then he remembered what Soames had said about Anne. Something about a friend in Port Said who could always use fresh talent.

He had spent too much time working in the Middle East himself to consider the remark merely an idle threat and he crossed to the window quickly and pulled back the curtain. The sash lifted easily and he looked out.

He was on the top floor of the house and the gardens lay forty feet below in the darkness. The nearest window was a good ten feet away to the left and impossible to reach.

He closed the window and moved back to the bed and considered the situation for a moment and then he crossed to the door and hammered on it with his bare fists.

After a while, steps hurried along the corridor and Karl said angrily. "Stop that row, Brady, or I'll come in and make you."

Brady renewed his attack on the door and the German swore fluently. "All right, you asked for it."

As the key clicked in the lock and the handle turned, Brady leaned against the door with all his weight. Karl cursed and shoved hard from the other side. Brady held him for a moment and then jumped back.

The door swung open with a crash and Karl staggered into the room and fell flat on his face, the .38 skidding across the floor.

He started to get up and Brady moved in fast and kicked him in the stomach. Karl subsided with a groan and Brady picked up the .38 and left the room, locking the door behind him.

He descended a flight of stairs to the next landing and recognized it at once. The office was at the far end and he stood outside and listened for a moment before turning the handle slowly.

She was reading some papers and a lamp cast a pool of light across the desk. Brady walked forward quietly and stood watching her from the shadows.

Some sixth sense must have warned her and she looked up sharply, looking oddly prim in horn-rimmed spectacles.

"Surprise, surprise!" he said softly.

She laid down her pen and said calmly, "What have you done with Karl?"

"He felt tired," Brady said. "So I left him to have a nice, long sleep."

She reached casually towards a drawer and he raised the .38 threateningly. "You do, and I'll put one right through your hand."

When she spoke, her voice was still calm, but a couple of deep lines had appeared between her eyes. "What do you want?"

"The girl will do for a start."

She lit a cigarette calmly and shook her head. "You're too late, lover. She's on board the *S.S. Kontoro* in the Pool of London and they go down-river in an hour."

"What game are you playing?" he said.

She shrugged. "No game. I told you I had to get rid of her, Brady. She knew too much."

"And this way you could make something on the transaction?"

"That's right, and there's nothing you can do about it—not a thing."

"Isn't there?" His voice was ice-cold and infinitely menacing. He reached forward and held the .38 six inches from her stomach. "If that boat goes before we can get her off, I'll put a bullet in your guts, I promise you. You're a big woman and you'll take a long time to go."

For the first time her composure broke. "You wouldn't dare."

"I've got nothing to lose," he said.

She got to her feet slowly. "I don't think I can get

(103)

ner back. I've already been paid my end by Captain Skiros and he expects to make something on the deal when he reaches Port Said."

"How much did you get?"

"Five hundred."

"You'd better get it and fast," he told her. "Time's running out."

She lifted a painting down from the wall and opened a small wall safe. After a moment she returned to the desk with a wad of five-pound notes held together by a rubber band.

He took the money from her and stuffed it into his pocket. "Now we go for a little drive. I've got a car outside. You can take the wheel."

"What happens when we reach the ship?"

He shrugged. "We'll play it as it comes."

"Skiros is a pretty hard apple, lover," she said. "He doesn't take kindly to people who try to lean on him."

"All you need to worry about is getting us on board," he said. "I'll handle the rest."

The house was quiet as they went downstairs. She got a coat from the cloakroom and Brady helped himself to a raincoat. They left by the side entrance.

The rain was falling heavily and slanting through the lamplight as they went down the drive and turned into the street. The car was still there. Brady unlocked the door quickly and she squeezed her massive bulk behind the wheel.

As he got in beside her, she said calmly, "What happens if the law stops us?"

"You'd better pray it doesn't," he said. "If they get me, they get you. That's a firm promise."

She shrugged, and moved into gear without replying. The roads were jammed with traffic and conditions were bad due to the early darkness and heavy rain, but she handled the wheel expertly and they made good time.

As they approached the docks, the streets became quieter until they were moving through dark canyons flanked by great warehouses, shuttered and barred for the night.

She braked to a halt underneath a lamp in a narrow alley beside a gate. Through the iron bars, he could see out into the river and somewhere, an anchor-chain rattled and a ship's hooter sounded faintly down-river.

"We'll have to walk from here," she said.

He got out and moved round to join her. The main gates were locked, but a small Judas gate at one side opened to her touch and they passed through.

The watchman's hut was dark and empty. "Where is he?" Brady demanded.

She shrugged. "Where he always is, I suppose. In the pub at the end of the street. He won't bother us."

As they rounded the corner of the first cargo shed, rain drifted in a cloud across the river, driven by the wind. Brady lowered his head to avoid the worst of it and followed her across the black shining cobbles to the ship which was moored at the far end of the wharf.

The *Kontoro* was brilliantly lit and hummed with the pulse-beat of her hidden machinery. The watchman who leaned over the rail and stared morosely out into the heavy rain, smoked a clay pipe and carried a pick helve.

Soames mounted the slippery gangplank and Brady followed her. "And who the hell might you be?" the watchman demanded ungraciously.

"I'm a friend of the captain's," she said. "I must see him before you sail. It's very urgent."

"No skin off my nose." The watchman shrugged. "He's in his cabin. You'd better hurry, though. We're casting-off in twenty minutes."

The decks bustled with activity as men worked busily, battening down hatch-covers and making ready to sail. Soames threaded her way through them, ignoring the ribald comments and coarse laughter, and mounted a companionway to the next deck.

At the entrance to the captain's cabin, she hesitated and turned to Brady. "What now?"

"Tell him you've changed your mind," Brady said. "I'll handle it from there."

When she opened the door, Skiros was sitting at a desk in one corner and he swivelled to face them, a pen in one hand. He was large and fat, the great pendulous stomach straining against the buttons of his shabby uniform. His face with its multiple chins gave an impression of jollity and good-humour that was belied by the sharp cunning in the little pig eyes.

He looked surprised and when he spoke, his English was good with just the hint of accent. "My dear professor, what brings you back so soon?"

Soames managed a smile. "Something came up, Skiros," she said. "Something important. I'm afraid I'm going to have to call our little deal off."

The smile remained fixed firmly in position, but his eyes became cold and hard. "But that is impossible, my friend. The bargain has been made. You have my money, I have the girl, so everybody should be satisfied."

"Not quite," Brady interrupted calmly. "The professor made a mistake. The merchandise wasn't hers to sell." He took the bundle of banknotes from his pocket and tossed them on to the desk.

Skiros laughed until his eyes almost disappeared between folds of flesh. "Your friend is really very funny," he said to Soames. "Does he expect me to give up the girl in exchange for what I paid for her? That would leave me with no profit on the transaction. In my country we do not do business in such a way."

"In my country we're not used to this kind of transaction so you'll have to excuse my bad manners." Brady produced the .38 from his raincoat pocket and thumbed back the hammer. "This thing has a hair trigger, fat man," he said. "I could easily have an accident. I probably will if you don't produce that girl in about ten seconds flat."

The Greek's eyes became round pieces of stone. "You are on my ship, surrounded by my crew," he said. "And they usually do as I tell them."

"In case you haven't noticed it, you've put on weight lately," Brady said calmly. "I'd find it difficult to miss."

"If I were you, I'd do as he says," Soames put in quickly. "He means every word, believe me."

Skiros sighed, put down his pen and took a bunch of keys from the drawer of his desk. "As always, I bow to your perspicacity, my friend. You will find, however that the terms of our next little transaction will require some adjusting, if only to recompense me for the loss of profit and considerable annoyance I have suffered over this affair."

He crossed to the door to the inner cabin and unlocked it. "Come out!" he said sharply and stood to one side.

Anne Dunning appeared in the doorway and stood there her shoulders bowed in defeat. Her face was shadowed so that the bones stood out in relief, the eyes deep-set in their sockets and the hand that pushed back a tendril of dark hair, trembled slightly.

Then she saw Brady, the shock was almost physical. She gave a long shuddering sigh and lurched forward into his arms.

Her slender body started to shake uncontrollably and he held her close with one hand and said, "Hang on, Anne. There's nothing to worry about any more. I'm going to get you out of here."

She nodded several times, unable to answer him and he glared coldly at Skiros. "What have you done to her?"

For the first time Skiros looked worried. "But nothing, I assure you, my friend. No one has laid a finger on her."

"I gave her an injection to keep her quiet earlier on this afternoon," Soames interrupted. "With some people it has side effects. Nothing serious. All she needs is a good night's sleep."

"Is that true, Anne?" Brady said. "This pig hasn't harmed you in any way?"

She nodded briefly and Brady turned to Soames, satisfied. "Okay, this is what we do. You go first with the girl. Skiros and I bring up the rear. If either of you makes a wrong move, he gets it. Is that understood?"

Skiros shrugged and reached for his cap. "How far do we go?"

"To the main gate," Brady said. "We've got a car there."

"I think you are a very careful man," Skiros said, and there was a reluctant smile on his face.

"If we parted at the gangplank, I'd have your crew on my tail before we'd gone halfway along the wharf. You know it and I know it," Brady said. "Now let's cut the small talk and move out."

Soames went first, supporting Anne easily with one massive arm and Skiros followed, Brady bringing up the rear. He had the .38 ready in his raincoat pocket, finger on the trigger, but there was no need—no need at all. As they negotiated the companionway and moved amongst the crew, heads lifted curiously, but Skiros made no sign. At the head of the gangplank he slapped the watchman on the shoulder and grinned. "Don't worry, I'm only going as far as the gate with my friends. Make ready to sail. We cast off as soon as I return."

No one spoke again until they reached the gates. Brady gave Soames the keys and she unlocked the door and put Anne into the rear seat. When this was accomplished, she got back behind the wheel and waited.

"May I go now?" the Greek said.

Brady nodded. "I don't see why not."

Skiros smiled and in the light of the lamp, his face looked quite genial. "Life is a circle, turning upon itself endlessly, my friend. We will meet again, and when we do . . ."

"It's hardly likely," Brady said. "We inhabit different worlds. I'd chalk it up to experience, if I were you, and leave it at that."

He climbed in beside Soames and she moved into gear and drove away. As she slowed to turn the corner at the end of the alley, Brady turned and looked through the rear window. The Greek was still standing there under the lamp, staring after them.

"You certainly know some lovely people," he said, lighting a cigarette.

They were moving along Aldgate and she braked to a halt on the opposite side of the road to the tube station. "Look, lover, you wanted your girl friend back and you've got her," she said. "If it's all the same to you, I'll drop off here and we'll call it square."

"Not quite," Brady said. "If I remember correctly, there was some question of a name, wasn't there?"

For a moment she glared at him defiantly, and then her shoulders sagged. "I wish I'd never set eyes on you, you bastard. The party you want is Jane Gordon. She has a flat at Carley Mansions, Baker Street."

"Where does she fit in?"

Soames shrugged wearily. "I don't know. She got in touch with me some days ago, said a friend of hers wanted to contact somebody reliable in Manningham. Someone who could keep his mouth shut. I owed her a favour from way back. I put her on to Das."

"But it was Haras who went to Manningham and gave Das his instructions," Brady said.

"So that was the way Jane wanted to handle it," Soames said. "It was no skin off my nose. After you came snooping round my place this morning, I got in touch with her by phone. Told her I had you under lock and key. She asked me to hang on to you for the time being. Said she had to get in touch with someone else. Someone important. Promised to phone me back at six tonight, but it's after that now."

"Carley Mansions, Baker Street," Brady said. He reached across her and opened the door. "If you haven't told me the truth, you'll be seeing me."

"What I've told you is strictly kosher, lover," she said. "I've had enough of you to last me a lifetime."

She scrambled out on to the pavement and made straight for the entrance to the tube station without looking back. Brady lit another cigarette and watched her, a slight frown on his face. He turned to Anne, who was leaning back in the corner of the seat, eyes closed. "Are you all right?"

She opened her eyes and nodded wearily. "I'm fine, just fine. I feel as if I could go to bed for a week, that's all."

"I'll be back in a couple of minutes," he said. "Then I'll take you straight home."

He got out of the car and walked across to the tube station. Just inside the entrance, there was a row of phone booths. Soames was in the end one, talking animatedly. He watched her for a moment, a tiny frown on his face, and then turned and hurried back to the car.

That she would get in touch with Jane Gordon was a chance he'd have to take. All it meant was that he would have to move much faster now.

Despite the poor weather, the West End was crowded as usual and it took him longer to reach Kensington than he had counted on. It was nearly eight o'clock when he braked to a halt outside the house in the quiet square.

Anne was a dead weight on his arm as he mounted

the stairs to the flat. The drug seemed to have taken even greater control and he carried her into the bedroom, half-fainting, and quickly stripped the clothes from her slim body.

She shivered slightly in the cool breeze from the window and he quickly pulled back the blankets and put her to bed. Her hair spread across the pillow, a dark halo round her head. She moaned once softly and he bent down and kissed her and then he quietly left the room.

There was a map of central London in the glove compartment of the car and he quickly located Baker Street. It was no more than fifteen minutes away by car and he drove through light traffic, past Kensington Gardens and out into the Bayswater Road. Some inner caution prompted him to park the car near Bond Street tube station and he went the rest of the way on foot.

Carley Mansions was an imposing block of flats at the Marylebone Road end of Baker Street. It looked extremely expensive. In a discreet gold-and-glass frame in the entrance there was a list of the residents. Miss Jane Gordon was listed as flat eight on the fourth floor.

Inside, a brocaded porter sat in a glass booth and read a magazine. As Brady watched, the telephone started to ring. The porter picked it up and turned wearily, leaning against the counter, his back to the entrance.

Brady didn't hesitate. He pushed open the heavy glass door, crossed the heavy carpet soundlessly, and went straight up the stairs.

The whole place looked very new and the sound-proofing was perfect. A stillness that was almost uncanny seemed to move ahead of him as he mounted to the fourth floor.

Flat eight was the last one in the corridor. He knocked lightly on the door and waited. There was no reply. He knocked again and tried the handle. The door opened smoothly before him.

The lights were on, but there was no one there. Several broad steps dropped down into a luxuriously furnished room, one side walled with glass, giving a magnificent view of London.

He could see through the serving hatch into the kitchen. It was in darkness, but the bedroom door was slightly open and the light was on.

It was the shoe he noticed first, lying in the middle of the carpet, slim and expensive, the stiletto heel somehow infinitely deadly.

The rest of her was sprawled on her face at the end of the bed, her dress rucked up wantonly, one slim hand clawing at the carpet. Someone had shot her in the back twice at close quarters with a parabellum from the look of the wounds.

She was only just dead, that much was obvious, and the faintly acrid taint of gunpowder still hung upon the air. He sighed heavily, crouched down and turned her over.

The sight of her face was like a heavy blow in the stomach, delivered low down, taking the breath from his body, for this wasn't Jane Gordon. *This was the woman he had known so briefly as Marie Duclos. The woman whose smashed and violated body he had last seen in the bedroom of her Chelsea apartment. The woman for whose murder he had been sentenced to death.*

For one single, terrifying moment, he thought he must be going mad, and then, quite suddenly, he was aware of the truth, or at least a part of it.

He started to get to his feet and behind him there was a quiet movement. Even as he turned, pulling the .38 from his pocket, a hand thudded solidly against the nape of his neck and he slumped forward on to his face with a cry of pain.

(9)

WHEN he opened his eyes again, he was sprawled on his face beside the body. There was only one added refinement. In his right hand he was firmly clutching a Mauser automatic with an SS bulbous silencer fitted to the barrel.

There was something familiar about it—something very familiar. It was the gun with which Anton Haras had tried to kill him in Manningham.

He could not have been unconscious for more than five minutes; that much was obvious. He scrambled to his feet, sat on the edge of the bed and massaged his neck muscles.

What a fool he'd been. What a blind, stupid fool. The smell of the gunpowder fresh on the air, the warmth of her body. It had been so obvious that she had only been dead for minutes. Perhaps the fatal shots had been fired as he was coming up the stairs and he had walked straight in like a lamb to the slaughter.

One thing was certain. If the police caught him here, he was finished, which was obviously what Haras had intended. This time it would mean the death cell plus all the trimmings, right up to the bitter end one cold, grey morning.

The room had been turned upside down, drawers pulled out, clothing scattered everywhere. It was hardly likely the Hungarian had overlooked anything incriminating.

Brady moved out quickly into the other room. As he mounted the steps to the door, he paused. Draped across a chair, was a woman's light raincoat and underneath it was her handbag. Obviously she had intended going out. Perhaps only the arrival of Haras had prevented her.

He emptied the bag on to the floor quickly and scattered its contents with one hand. There were a couple of banknotes, some coins, lipstick, jewelled powder compact and car keys.

There was also a letter, newly opened, the stamp bearing the postmark of the day. It was addressed in neat angular handwriting to Miss Jane Gordon, Carley Mansions, Baker Street, and he took out the single sheet of paper quickly and examined it.

It was the briefest of notes. *Dear Jane, looking forward to seeing you tonight. I'll be free from nine o'clock onwards. Your loving mother.*

But it was the printed address at the head of the notepaper which he found most interesting. *2 Edgbaston Square,* Chelsea. Marie Duclos had lived in

Edgbaston Gardens. Now what was that supposed to mean?

For a moment he remembered the street lined with narrow Victorian houses with the graveyard and the church at the end and something elemental stirred inside him, lifting the hair on the nape of his neck. It was as if he was afraid—afraid to return to that place.

He shrugged it off with a grim laugh and opened the door. Whatever happened, he was going back there. He had no choice.

When he reached the hall, the porter was still drowsing over his magazine. Brady crossed to the door quickly and was already disappearing into the night as the man glanced up.

As he hurried along the pavement, a bell sounded shrilly on the night, and a police car swung round the corner from the Marylebone Road and braked to a halt in front of Carley Mansions.

Brady kept on walking, quickening his pace slightly. He turned into the bustle of Oxford Street a couple of minutes later, got into the car and drove away.

There was a taste of fog in the air, that typical London fog that drifts up from the Thames, yellow and menacing, wrapping the city in its shroud.

At least it made things easier for him. He passed a policeman standing on a corner by a crossing, moisture streaming from his cape. Brady braked to a halt to let someone cross over and the policeman waved him on. Brady grinned. What was it Joe Evans used to say? *The best place to hide from a copper is right under his bleeding nose.*

They were probably watching the boats more than

anything else, thinking he might try to get back to the States. He passed into Sloane Square and a few moments later, braked to a halt on the Embankment on the opposite side of the road to the spot where it had all begun.

He stood under the same lamp, lit a cigarette and stared down at the river and for a single moment, time had no meaning—no meaning at all.

He turned away and crossed the road and walked along the opposite pavement through the thickening fog. Rain dripped depressingly from the trees and most of the leaves had gone. He paused on the corner and looked up at the old blue-and-white enamel plate that said Edgbaston Gardens, and then moved on.

The road repairs had long since been finished and the house was shuttered and dark. He gazed up at it, thinking about what had happened there, seeing the crowd tight against the railings, the man who had panicked like some hunted animal, with his back to the wall as they moved in on him. The beginning of a long nightmare.

He passed the railings of the graveyard, beaded with moisture, silent and waiting. The church stood on a corner plot and out of some strange sixth sense he knew what he was going to find when he turned into the next street and examined the name plate. Edgbaston Square and number two was next to the church.

He mounted the steps to the door. There was a light on in the porch and a neat card in a black metal frame said *Madame Rose Gordon—visits by appointment only*.

A car was parked a few yards away and as he turned to look at it, he was aware of movement inside the house. He descended the steps quickly and melted into the shadows.

The door opened and a woman in a fur coat moved out into the porch. She turned and spoke to someone inside. "You've helped me more than I can say, my dear Madame Rose. I can't wait to see you again next week."

Brady couldn't catch the reply, but the door closed and the woman in the fur coat descended the steps and walked to the car. A moment later she drove away.

He stood there, for a minute, looking up at the house, a frown on his face and then he turned and walked back along the front of the church and went in through the main gate.

The windows were like strips of rainbow in the night, misty and ill-defined like an impressionist painting and an organ sounded faintly. The tower was cocooned in a network of steel scaffolding and he skirted a heap of rubble and moved round to the back.

He found the garden of Madame Rose's house with no difficulty. It was separated from the graveyard by a six-foot stone wall, at one end of which there was a narrow wooden door.

It was locked. He tried it tentatively and then turned and picked his way through the gravestones to the other side. As he approached the garden at the rear of Marie Duclos's house, a quiet voice said, "Excuse me, but can I do anything for you?"

He turned quickly. Standing in the patch of light thrown out by the side windows of the church was an old white-haired man in a shabby tweed jacket, his neck encircled by the stiff white collar of a priest.

Brady moved towards him with a ready smile. "I know it must sound pretty crazy, but to tell you the truth I was looking for a headstone. I always understood my great-grandfather was buried somewhere in this churchyard."

"Ah, an American," the old priest said. "Well, I don't think you'll have much luck tonight. Much better to come back tomorrow. As a matter of fact I'll be here myself in the morning. I could check in the parish register for you."

Brady tried to put real regret into his voice. "It's kind of you to offer, but I'm afraid I'm flying out again tomorrow." He laughed lightly. "At least I've managed to see the church which is something."

"It is rather lovely, isn't it?" the old man said and there was real enthusiasm in his voice. "Of course it was hit by a bomb during the war. That's one reason for the scaffolding round the tower. We can't put off the repairs any longer, but there are many features of interest."

"It's a pity I'm not staying longer," Brady said. "I could have attended one of your services."

"But I'm afraid that would have been quite out of the question," the old man said. "Ever since that bomb, the old place has been in such a shaky condition, we've never felt able to take the risk of allowing a congregation inside. I'm at another church now, not far away, but I like to visit here from time to time to keep the organ in trim and so on." He sighed. "I suppose they'll sell the site one of these days."

"I noticed a gate in the wall leading into the garden of a house at the rear," Brady said. "Was that the vicarage?"

The old man shook his head. "No, that used to be the sexton's house." He pointed across to the house in Edgbaston Gardens. "That used to be the vicarage."

Brady tried to keep his voice steady. "I was having a drink in the pub round the corner and asking my way here. The landlord told me there was a shocking murder committed near the church some months ago."

"Yes, I'm afraid so," the priest said. "A dreadful affair. The victim was a young woman who had the upstairs apartment in the old vicarage. It was all most distressing."

"I'm sure it must have been," Brady said. He turned and looked across at the house. "There's one thing puzzles me. The sexton had a short-cut to the church through the gate in his garden wall, but you didn't. That must have been very inconvenient."

"Oh, but I did," the priest assured him. "You wouldn't notice it in the dark; in fact you'd have to look twice in daylight to see it. There's a gate set in the railings at the end of the garden. I was only noticing the other day, it's almost completely blocked with rhododendron bushes. I don't suppose it's been used for years."

"No, I don't suppose it has." They were back at the front of the church and Brady pulled up his collar against a sudden flurry of rain. "Well, I've imposed on your time for too long. I really must be going."

The old man smiled. "Not at all, it's been a pleasure talking to you. I'm only sorry you haven't got time to come back tomorrow."

Brady went down the path quickly and behind him, the door opened and closed again. The rain was falling softly through the sickly yellow glow of the street lamp as he turned into Edgbaston Square and mounted the steps to number two. He pressed the bell-push and waited.

Steps shuffled along the corridor inside and he could see a shadowy figure through the frosted glass. The door clicked and opened a few inches and an old woman looked out at him.

Her hair was drawn back in a tight, old-fashioned bun, the face old and wrinkled, long jet ear-rings hanging down on either side. It was a face he had seen before, peering from behind the door of the downstairs apartment on the night Marie Duclos was murdered.

He kept well back in the shadows. "Madame Rose?" he said.

She nodded. "That's right." Her voice was old and strangely lifeless, like dry, dead leaves whispering through a forest in the evening.

"I wonder if you could spare me a few moments of your time?"

"You wish to consult the stars?"

He nodded. "That's right. I was told you could help me."

"I only take clients by appointment, young man," she said. "I have to be very careful. The police are most strict in these matters."

"I'm only in London for a brief visit," he told her, keeping to the same formula. "I'm flying out in the morning."

She sighed. "Oh, very well, but I can only spare you half an hour. I'm expecting a visitor."

The hall was gloomy and oak-panelled. He waited

for her to close the door and when she turned and looked up at him she frowned slightly. "Your face seems strangely familiar. Are you sure we've never met?"

"I'm an American," he said. "This is my first visit to England."

"I must be mistaken."

She led the way along the corridor, pulled back a dark velvet drape and opened a heavy door.

The room into which they entered was strangely subdued, cut-off from the street by heavy curtains, the only light a single lamp on a small table. There was a fake electric log fire in the hearth and the room was unpleasantly warm. Brady unbuttoned his raincoat and sat down at the table.

The old woman sat opposite him, several books at her elbow, a pad of blank paper before her. She picked up a pencil. "Give me your date of birth, the place and the exact time. The time is most important, so please be accurate."

He told her and looked over her shoulder into the shadows crowding out of the corners, beating against the pool of light thrown out by the lamp. He wondered what he was going to say next, but decided to wait until she gave him an opening.

She consulted several books, making quick notes on the pad and finally grunted. "Do you believe in astrology, young man?"

"I wouldn't be here if I didn't," he said.

She nodded. "You are ambidextrous?"

It was more a statement of fact than a question and he said in some surprise, "Yes, that's right. How did you know?"

"Many of those born under the sign of Scorpio are," she said and consulted her notes. "Life for you is often a battleground."

"You can say that again," Brady told her.

She nodded calmly. "Mars, Sun and Neptune in conjunction on the mid-heaven will result in a certain sharpness of tongue and temper. Your map shows signs of a dangerous, almost explosive, tendency to violence in your character. You tend to regard everyone you meet with suspicion. You are your own worst enemy."

Brady sat back in his chair and harsh laughter erupted from his mouth. "I think that's bloody marvellous."

The old woman looked across at him, eyes glinting in the lamplight. "You appear to find something humorous in what I have just said, young man."

"And that's the understatement of the age," Brady replied.

She carefully piled her books one on top of the other and gathered her papers. "Who did you say recommended me to you?"

"I didn't," Brady said, "But as a matter of fact, it was your daughter, Jane Gordon."

"Indeed?" the old woman frowned. "We shall see. I'm expecting her to arrive at any moment."

"You'll have to wait a long time, Mrs. Gordon," he said calmly. "She's dead."

Her face seemed to wither before his very eyes, to wrinkle into a yellowing sheet of parchment. Her hand went up to her mouth and she coughed convulsively and then she started to choke horribly.

Brady moved round to her side and noticed that she

was tugging at the handle of a drawer with one hand. He jerked it open and found a small glass phial of white tablets. There was water on the sideboard. He filled a glass quickly and brought it back to her and she forced two of the tablets into her mouth and washed them down.

After a moment, she sighed and a dry sob bubbled up from her throat. "My heart," she said. "Must be careful about sudden shocks."

"I'm sorry," he said. "It isn't the sort of news one can wrap up in pretty paper with a pink ribbon, not the way it happened."

The strange thing was that she appeared to accept the fact that he was telling the truth without question. "Who killed her?"

"A man called Haras," Brady said. "Anton Haras. Do you know him?"

"I know him," she said, nodding her head, the black eyes staring into the darkness. "I know him." She turned and looked straight at him. "Who are you, young man?"

"Matthew Brady," he said simply.

"Ah, yes," she said softly. "I think I knew that you would come, a long time ago."

"You were there in the house that night, weren't you?" he said. "Who was the man with your daughter?"

"Miklos Davos," she said in a whisper.

Brady frowned. "You mean the oil-king?"

She nodded. "Some people say he is the richest man in the world, Mr. Brady. I only know that he is the most evil."

"Tell me what happened that night," Brady said.

Remembering, her voice seemed to be on another plane. "My daughter was engaged in a shameful trade, Mr. Brady. She was a Madame, a brothel-keeper, call it what you will. She had much property in her name, most of which really belonged to Davos."

"Was she in love with him?"

"Love?" The old woman laughed harshly. "She was completely under his influence. For her, he could do no wrong. For his sake, she produced a succession of young women to satisfy his morbid desires to inflict pain. He was a brutal and perverted sadist, ceaselessly searching for new sensation."

"And where did Marie Duclos fit in?"

The old woman shrugged. "She was a French girl he took a particular fancy to, I don't know why. She was installed in the upstairs apartment and the other tenant removed. For two months he visited her ceaselessly."

"By way of the churchyard?" Brady said.

She shook her head. "No, he only used that method during the week that the road was being repaired. He didn't want the nightwatchman to see him entering the house."

"But why did he kill the girl?"

"She tried to blackmail him. A foolish thing to do—he was liable to the most insane rages. When he came for my daughter that night, I followed them back through the churchyard and listened while he told her what he had done. Her only worry was that he might come to harm."

"What did you do?" Brady said.

She shrugged. "What could I do? I'm an old woman and I was listening to a daughter who had become a stranger to me. He told her there was a way out, that all they needed was a scapegoat to satisfy the police. They didn't need to look far with the Embankment at the bottom of the street. The first drunk on the first bench would do."

"And that happened to be me," Brady said bitterly.

A slight breeze touched the back of his neck and the door creaked. He turned slowly, his hand sliding into his raincoat pocket and a familiar voice said, "Please to stand very still, Mr. Brady."

Haras moved into the room, the lamplight glinting on his spectacles. Brady raised his arms slowly and the Hungarian removed the Mauser and slipped it into his pocket.

"Now you may put down your arms."

He was holding the .38 and there was a confident smile on his face. "Sorry I've been delayed, but I was caught in a traffic jam in Oxford Street and missed you. I was waiting outside Carley Mansions, by the way. It was quite depressing to see you scuttle out ahead of the police, but somehow, I *thought* you might be coming here. You've really done quite well, Brady."

"For the first drunk on the first bench," Brady said bitterly.

"So, the old goat has been opening her mouth, has she?" The Hungarian smiled genially. "We'll have to do something about that."

He was standing well back from the table, a confident smile on his face. Madame Rose glared up at him fixedly. "You filthy swine," she said and started to get to her feet.

"Stay where you are!" Haras ordered.

As the Hungarian's eyes flickered to the old woman, Brady scized the lamp and pulled it from its socket, plunging the room into darkness.

Haras fired twice and the old woman screamed and crumpled to the floor. She lay in the patch of light thrown out by the electric fire and blood poured over her face from a gaping wound in the forehead.

Brady crouched for a moment at the side of a large wing-backed chair and then started to crawl round the back of the old-fashioned horse-hair sofa, making for the door.

Haras was still standing by the table and Brady could see the dark bulk of him in the slight glow of the electric fire.

"You can't get away, Brady," he said. "You don't stand a chance. I've got both the guns."

Brady remembered there had been four rounds in the .38 and Haras had fired two of them. He crouched between a chair and the wall a couple of yards from the door and carefully lifted a small china cat from a coffee-table beside him.

"I'm running out of patience, Brady," Haras said and there was an edge of anger in his voice.

Brady lobbed the cat across the room into the far corner. As it smashed against the wall, the Hungarian turned and fired twice in rapid succession. Brady jumped for the door, wrenched it open and darted along the corridor to the rear of the house.

Behind him there was a cry of rage. He ran into a large kitchen and made straight for the door at the far end. It was locked and as he fumbled desperately with the key, he heard the peculiar muffled cough of the silenced Mauser and a bullet scattered splinters of wood above his head.

He got the door open and went down a flight of steps two at a time into the garden. Ahead of him loomed the high wall and beyond it was the church-yard.

When he paused at the little wicker gate, Haras was already halfway along the path. Brady raised his foot and stamped twice at the gate, splintering the flimsy wood around the lock. As the Mauser coughed again, he was through and crouching as he ran between the gravestones.

Light still drifted out through the great windows, staining the thickening fog in vivid colours and he dodged behind a high tomb and listened. There was no sound and after a moment or two, he moved between the gravestones, keeping his head down, skirted the base of the tower, and paused.

The organ was playing again, muted and far away. Brady could feel the sweat on his face. The drive stretched before him, the gate to the street stood open. He moved forward and Haras stepped out from behind a flying buttress ten yards away, the lamplight glinting on his spectacles.

The Hungarian had obviously circled the church from the other side. As he raised the Mauser, Brady stepped back into the darkness at the base of the tower and started to climb the network of steel scaffolding.

Within a few moments, the fog had swallowed him and he made good progress, swinging expertly from pole to pole. Within a couple of minutes, he heaved himself up on to a narrow catwalk and realized there was no farther to go.

He stood there, ears strained for the slightest sound. There was a long silence and a cold wind lifted through the fog, chilling him so that he shivered despite himself.

He started to work his way along the catwalk and then suddenly, a board creaked and Haras said softly, "I know you're there, Brady."

The Mauser coughed, the bullet whispering away into the night and Brady moved back carefully, removing his raincoat at the same time.

As he got the coat off, his foot caught against a length of iron piping which rolled across the catwalk and disappeared over the edge.

Haras moved forward quickly, arm outstretched. He fired once, the bullet ricocheting from a steel stanchion, and Brady tossed the raincoat into his face. The Hungarian gave a muffled cry of alarm, staggered back, and stepped off the end of the catwalk into space. For one frozen second he seemed suspended in mid-air and then the fog swallowed him up.

Brady's hands were shaking and his shirt was damp with his sweat, but without hesitating, he went over the edge of the catwalk and started to climb down.

Haras lay on his back in the path, a good fifteen or twenty yards from the base of the tower and the old priest knelt beside him. He looked up as Brady approached.

"Is he dead?" Brady said.

The old man nodded. "I'm afraid so."

The Hungarian's eyeballs had retracted and he stared sightlessly up at Brady, blood on his mouth. "He killed a woman a few minutes ago," Brady said.

"Back there in what used to be the sexton's old house."

The old priest got to his feet slowly. "You mean Mrs. Gordon? But why?" He moved closer and stared up into Brady's face and something clicked. "You're Matthew Brady, aren't you? You're the man the police are looking for. I saw your picture in the paper to-night."

Brady turned and walked away quickly. Once in the street, he started to run.

A few moments later, he was driving away.

(10)

MIKLOS DAVOS lived in Mayfair, he got that much from the directory of the first phone booth he came to. When he went back to the car, his hands were still trembling and he lit a cigarette before driving away.

By now the old priest would have got in touch with the police and they would know that he was on the loose in London. Once they had connected the deaths of Jane Gordon, her mother, and Haras, the hunt would be up with a vengeance.

He had only one chance. To get to Davos, to squeeze the truth out of him, because he was the only person left on earth who knew the real facts.

As he took the car expertly through the heavy traffic, he tried to remember what he knew about Davos. It wasn't very much.

He was of Hungarian extraction, which explained the link-up with Haras. A strange enigmatic figure, he shunned publicity like the plague. It was said that he virtually controlled the oil-supply of the Western world. A ruthless man, an empire-builder who crushed all opposition mercilessly.

Brady's jaw tightened as he turned the car into a quiet street off Park Lane. Perhaps it was time some-one cut Mr. Davos down to size.

The houses were Georgian and beautifully restored. There seemed to be a party going on and parked cars stretched in a line down one side of the street.

Davos lived at number twenty. Brady found space for the car and then mounted the steps to the front door and pressed the bell-push.

He could hear laughter from somewhere inside and music and after a moment or two, there was a protest-ing curse on the other side of the door and it was flung back with a crash against the wall.

The man who faced him was very drunk. He was wearing a corduroy jacket and fringe beard and his eyes were wet blobs in the pale face.

"Well, if you intend to stand there all night, old man, that suits me fine," he said cheerfully and turned away.

The corridor was dimly lit by candles. A tremen-dous hubbub from the far end indicated the vortex of the party although delighted cries and fast beat music sounded from a room on his right as he passed.

He entered the room at the end of the corridor and found himself on the edge of a noisy articulate throng. Everybody seemed to be talking to everybody else at the tops of their voices. The windows were blacked out and the light came from candles stuck into old wine bottles and placed at various strategic points around the room.

Brady was puzzled. This wasn't the sort of party he would have expected a man like Miklos Davos to give. It took him straight back to the old days, living in Greenwich Village when he was a student at Columbia. The men seemed to have longer hair than the girls and most of them sported beards.

The bar was an improvised affair in one corner and consisted of planks laid across a couple of beer barrels. The barman seemed to be having a hard time keeping up with the demand and Brady helped himself to a beer and moved away.

On the whole, the crowd was an unsavoury bunch and most of them were already drunk and spoiling for mischief. Somebody was trying to stand on his hands on a table and drink a glass of beer at the same time. There was a delighted roar from the crowd as he lost his balance and Brady, turning away, was pushed hard against a young girl, knocking the glass from her hand.

"I'm sorry," he said. "I'll get you another. What was it?"

"Oh, that's all right. I'd rather have a cigarette if you've got one," she said.

She couldn't have been more than seventeen, her face round and unformed and pale with excitement as she looked around her.

He gave her a cigarette and she lit it inexpertly. "Isn't this marvellous?" she said brightly.

"Just great," Brady assured her. "Who's giving the party, anyway?"

Her eyes went round with surprise. "You mean to say you don't know?"

He grinned. "I just got into town. Some friends of

mine were invited so they brought me with them. It all happened in something of a rush."

"That explains it," she said. "Lucia's giving the party. Lucia Davos. Haven't you ever met her?"

He shook his head. "I don't think so. I've only just got over here from the States."

"Oh, an American?" The girl smiled. "She'll like that. If you want to meet her, you'll find her in the other room singing with the band."

A hand reached out, grabbed her by the arm and the crowd swallowed her. Brady pushed his way through to the door and went along the corridor to the other room. As he paused in the doorway, a young maid in black-and-white uniform moved past him, her tray piled high with empty glasses. There were dark smudges of fatigue under her eyes and he felt a momentary pang of sympathy as a drunk stumbled against her, sending several glasses tumbling to the floor.

Brady picked them up quickly and replaced them on the tray. "You don't look too good," he said. "Can you manage?"

She smiled up at him gratefully. "Don't worry about me. They've had it. I'm going to put my feet up in the kitchen and have a smoke and a cup of tea."

She turned away and Brady went into the front room. A three-piece combo played softly, but with a beat and a girl sat on the piano, legs crossed, and sang a low, throaty blues.

She didn't really have much of a voice, but there was something there, a touch of the night, perhaps. A dying fall. The little girl who had been born to everything and had found already that she had nothing.

With her cropped hair and lack of make-up, the slim, boyish figure in the knitted dress looked strangely sexless. When she finished, there was scattered applause and someone shouted, "Another one, Lucia!"

She shook her head. "Maybe later. I need a drink."

She slid down to the floor and the combo started to play good and loud, the sounds reverberating from the walls. There was a tray of Martinis on a table near the wall and Brady took one and pushed his way towards her.

She was leaning on the piano, beating time with one hand. When he offered her the drink, she turned to thank him, and a slight frown creased her brow. "I don't know you," she said.

"I came with a crowd," he told her. "I like your song. I think you've really got something."

Her eyes were slightly glazed and he knew that she had already had too much to drink. "You an American?" she demanded.

He nodded. "Just got in today."

She was still frowning, eyeing him up and down. After a moment she said, "I know what's wrong with you. You are the only man in the room wearing a suit."

Brady glanced round quickly. The strange thing was that she was right. He stuck out like a sore thumb. "Who did you say you came with?" she demanded.

"Okay, Miss Davos," he said and shrugged as if giving in. "I suppose I'd better come clean. I was hoping for an interview with your father."

"A newspaperman." She swallowed her Martini. "I thought it was something like that. Well, you're wasting your time. My father never gives interviews. In any case, he's out of town."

"Perhaps if you could tell me where he is," Brady persisted. "He might be willing to make an exception. It would be a real scoop for me."

She looked straight at him and said in her dry, remote voice, "Look, you're beginning to bore me. If I were you, I'd finish my drink and leave."

She turned away as the music lifted to a crescendo and Brady faded into the anonymity of the crowd. He slipped out through the door and moved back into the other room, his mind working desperately. Somehow, he had to find where Davos had gone, but how?

There was a sudden roar and a girl was lifted up on to the bar. Someone started to clap rhythmically and the crowd took it up. The girl was handsome in a bold, sluttish way and obviously very drunk. She started to strip.

There was no great artistry in her performance. She simply took off her clothes as if she was getting ready for bed and threw each article to the delighted crowd. As she started to unfasten her brassière, Brady turned away. He stood there in the corridor, oblivious to the roar of the crowd, and then he remembered the maid.

It was worth trying and he moved into the side corridor that led to the rear of the house. He opened a door and found himself in a large, well-lighted kitchen.

The maid was sitting in front of the stove, legs stretched out, a cigarette in one hand. She turned in surprise and then a slight smile touched her mouth. "Oh, it's you. Looking for a cup of tea?"

Brady grinned and lit a cigarette. "I wouldn't mind. A bit too noisy in there for my liking."

She filled another cup, added milk and sugar and handed it to him. "To tell you the truth, I thought you didn't look as if you were enjoying yourself back there."

He smiled ruefully. "The trouble is, I'm not here to enjoy myself. I'm a newspaper man. My editor told me to get an interview with Miklos Davos or else. That's why I gate-crashed the party."

"Mr. Davos at one of his daughter's parties?" she chuckled. "That'll be the day. He never gives interviews, anyway."

"Have you any idea where he is now?"

She nodded. "He went down to the island this morning. Made up his mind just like that. Had us all running round in circles."

"The island?" Brady said.

"Shayling Island," she explained "It's about two miles off the Essex coast near a fishing village called Harth. He has a house there."

"What's it like?" Brady said.

She shuddered. "Gloomy sort of place. I spent a few weeks there last summer when he had guests. It always seemed to be raining." As Brady put down his cup she got to her feet. "But you're wasting your time. He won't see you, even if you go down there."

"Oh, you never know," Brady said lightly. "I might catch him on a good day."

"He never has good days," she said cryptically.

"Thanks for the tea," he said, "and the information. You've probably saved my job."

"I wouldn't be too sure of that," she said and he grinned and closed the door.

By now, the party had really started to fan out and there seemed to be noise and disturbance echoing from every corner of the house. He could still hear it clearly on the night air as he went down the front steps to the car and drove away.

The fog had thickened so that at times, traffic was reduced to a crawl, but it still only took him half an hour to get to that quiet square in Kensington.

He parked the car and went upstairs quickly. When he opened the door, the apartment was in darkness. He stood outside Anne's door for a moment, listening to her steady breathing before moving into the kitchen.

He felt surprisingly hungry and started to make a bacon-and-egg fry. As he scooped it from the pan to plate, there was a slight noise behind him and he turned to see her standing in the doorway.

She was tightening the cord of a housecoat, her hair straggling across her face, the eyes still swollen and full of sleep.

"Would you like something to eat?" he said.

She shook her head. "Just coffee."

He poured coffee into a cup for her, strong and black with plenty of sugar and she sat on the opposite side of the table and watched him eat.

All at once, there was an intimacy between them, a definite feeling that this was how it always should be. Brady sensed it and realized that she did also, but it remained unspoken.

She smiled gently. "You look tired."

"It's been a hard night," he said.

"Did you manage to find this Jane Gordon person the Soames woman told you about when we were in the car?"

"I'm afraid I was too late," he said, "but I found what I needed to know in the end."

He lit a cigarette and gave her a brief outline of the events of the past few hours. When he had finished, she sat there without saying a word, staring sombrely into space.

"What do you think?" he said.

"I think you should go to the police," she said. "I think things have gone far enough."

"But Davos is the one person left on earth who knows the truth," he said. "Do you think it's likely he'll make a confession at this stage?"

She frowned, her fingers twisting together nervously. "But what about the others who've been mixed up in this affair? Das and Professor Soames, for examples. The police should be able to get something out of them."

He shook his head. "Not a chance. Even Soames didn't know who Jane Gordon was working for. My one hope is to get to Davos, to force him to confess before the police lay me by the heels."

"And what if he refuses?" she demanded. "What will you do then? Kill him?"

"And why not?" he said bitterly. "If ever a man deserved to die, he does."

He got to his feet and paced restlessly across the floor. After a moment he turned back to the table. She sat with her head bowed and he pulled her to her feet and held her close in his arms. "I lost control there for a moment. I'm sorry. I'm tired. I suppose we both are. Better go to bed."

"The man who handled your case before," she said. "This Inspector Mallory. Couldn't he do something?"

"He certainly did a hell of a lot for me last time," Brady said. He led her through the living-room and back into her bedroom. "Now forget about it. We'll talk it over in the morning."

"What about you?" she said.

He shrugged. "I'll manage on the divan in the living-room."

She got into bed, but her face was still strained and anxious. "You will go to the police, won't you, Matt?"

"Sure I will." He leaned down and kissed her.

The last thing he remembered was her smile, warm and wonderful as he switched out the light and gently closed the door.

(11)

HE went into the kitchen, had another coffee and waited for her to go to sleep. It didn't take long. He stood outside her door and listened and then he pulled on his jacket and went back into the kitchen.

He managed to find a memo pad and pencil and sat down at the table to write her a note. After two attempts, he crumpled the paper into a ball and tossed it into a corner. There was really nothing left to say.

It was almost two a.m. when he closed the door of the apartment and went quietly downstairs.

He unlocked the car, took the road map from the glove compartment and left the keys in its place. There was a good chance he would never get out of London and when they caught him, he didn't want to be in Anne's car. He'd involved her too much already.

The fog had reduced visibility to thirty or forty yards and he walked briskly along the pavement, his senses alert for danger.

He had his first break half an hour later in a side street near the Albert Hall. A small and battered van was parked in a cul-de-sac. The lock on the door was already broken, but the owner had taken the key with him. Brady climbed in and reached behind the dashboard. He tore the ignition wires free and joined them together. A few minutes later he was driving cautiously away.

He stopped a little while later in a quiet side street and consulted the map. Essex was a county he knew reasonably well. Only three years previously he had been engineer in charge of a bridge project near Chelmsford.

Harth was near the tip of a spur of the coastline that jutted out where the River Blackwater emptied into the North Sea. It seemed to be a sparsely inhabited area with few roads. As the young maid had told him, Shayling Island was about two miles off-shore.

He stuffed the map into his pocket and drove away. According to the fuel gauge, there were only a couple of gallons in the tank, but for the moment, he concentrated on his driving. Minor problems could wait till later.

There was a surprising amount of traffic still on the roads. Probably people who had been delayed by the fog, he decided. Once out of the centre of London, he kept to the back streets, working in the direction of Romford, finally coming out on to the Chelmsford road.

Once past Romford he relaxed, lit a cigarette and concentrated on his driving. The fog was not as bad as it had been in London, but bad enough and it was a full hour before he turned off the main road and lost himself in a maze of back-country lanes.

He stopped frequently to consult the map and passed through several villages until finally, he took a wrong turning. As the first cold light of dawn crept through the fog, he drove through Southminster.

He followed the road to Tillingham for another half-mile and then the engine seemed suddenly to lose power, coughed once asthmatically, and died.

The fuel gauge still indicated two gallons which didn't prove a thing and he got out and had a look at the tank. There was still a little in there and he lifted the hood and examined the engine.

As he did so, a police constable rode out of the fog on a bicycle, cape swinging from his shoulders. He braked to a halt and propped the bike against the hedge before coming forward.

"Having a spot of bother?" he said cheerfully.

Brady kept his head down. "Nothing I can't handle, thank you."

What was it Joe Evans had called it? Lag's Luck. The unexpected that always happens to the man on the run?

"You're not from these parts, are you?" the constable said.

"No, just passing through," Brady told him.

There was a heavy pause before the man said, "I wonder if I might have a look at your driving licence, sir?"

"I'm afraid I haven't got it with me right now," Brady said.

The engine suddenly coughed into life again and he quickly pulled down the hood. "I guess that fixes it."

As he moved towards the van door, the constable caught hold of his arm and jerked him round. "Now, just a minute, sir. I'm afraid I'll . . ." The words died away as a look of complete astonishment passed across his face. "You're Brady," he said stupidly. "Matthew Brady."

The engine stopped again and somehow there was something utterly final about it. There was a moment of complete stillness and then, as the fingers started to tighten on his arm, Brady struck out wildly at the big, genial face and ran into the fog.

Once out of sight, he forced his way through the hedge and ran across a ploughed field. He came to a fence, clambered over, and kept on going. After he had covered half a mile, he stopped and slumped down to the ground under a tree in a small copse.

There was no sound of pursuit, he hadn't really expected any. By now the constable would be at the nearest telephone, nursing his smashed mouth and passing on his news to his superiors. Within an hour, two at the most, every able-bodied man in the district would be looking for him and he was trapped. Trapped with his back to the sea. His one chance was to reach Harth, steal a boat and reach Shayling Island.

He started to walk, but the fog was so thick that he lost his sense of direction completely after the first hour. He didn't feel tired, but there was a slight ache in his legs and his stomach felt empty.

He finally decided to have a rest and sat down under a tree and smoked his last cigarette. A small wind lifted through the trees, bringing with it a good salt smell of the sea. A sudden thrill ran through him and he scrambled to his feet. If he kept on walking straight into the wind, he would come to the shore. After that, he only had to follow the coastline to reach Harth.

He started forward and there was a sudden cry from somewhere on his left. He turned, crouching, as three men emerged from the fog and paused on the edge of the trees.

"Stand where you are!" one of them called.

As Brady turned to run, a shotgun roared and lead pellets sang through the trees above his head. Behind him a dog barked excitedly, but he kept on going, scrambled over a fence and found himself ankle-deep in marsh water.

As he progressed, it grew deeper until he was floundering knee-deep, the brown water churning about his knees. He kept on moving over to his left, pausing occasionally to listen to the cries of his pursuers, but finally they faded and he was alone.

He could hear the waves breaking on the shore long before he saw them and then he came up out of the marsh, over a small sand dune and down on to the shore.

He started to trot along the wet sand as rain began to fall, lightly at first, and then with increasing force. Soon the fog started to lift.

He was beginning to feel tired and once he fell. When he got up, his legs were trembling slightly but he forced himself to break into a stumbling trot again.

His mouth was dry and there was a slight ache somewhere behind his right eye, but he kept on going because he had no choice. The hounds were in full cry now. It was with a sense of shock that he found himself knee-deep in water. At this point the sand ended and the sea swept in close against jagged rocks.

On the other side of them stood a boathouse stoutly constructed of weathered grey stone with a slipway running clear into green water.

A headland jutted out on the other side of the tiny cove and beyond it, chimney smoke lifted into the grey morning. When he turned and looked out to sea, there was Shayling Island, half-veiled in a curtain of rain.

He slid down the rocks knee-deep into water and plunged towards the slipway. The wooden door of the boathouse wasn't padlocked, but he hadn't expected it to be. Fishing communities were the same the world over. Boats were never kept under lock and key. Emergencies were too frequent.

He opened the doors wide and moved inside. There was a heavy fishing cobble which needed at least three men to handle it satisfactorily, but at one side, he found a small sailing dinghy.

The wind was freshening, lifting the waves into white-caps as he ran the dinghy down into the water and stepped the mast. The sail billowed out as soon as he unfurled it and the dinghy heeled slightly and water poured over the gunn'l. He adjusted his weight to compensate and a moment later, moved out of the cove into the North Sea.

He had last sailed a dinghy off Cape Cod during long summer holidays as a boy, but never in weather like this. The light craft wasn't built for it and bucked wildly over the waves, shipping water constantly.

Within a short time he was soaked to the skin and bitterly cold. He hung on desperately to the tiller as the wind freshened and the waves began to chop menacingly.

Through the curtain of rain, the island loomed larger. Great cliffs lifted out of the sea and at their feet, the waves rolled in to dash upon jagged, dangerous-looking rocks.

There was no sign of a landing place. He tried to trim the sail to follow the shoreline, but the wind was too strong for him and suddenly, the cliffs were no more than a hundred yards away.

He dropped the sail hurriedly and reached for the oars, but it was too late. He was caught in a giant hand and carried helplessly in.

Strange, swirling currents twisted him in a circle and there was a hollow, slapping sound against the keel of the boat. At one side, the water broke suddenly, white spray foaming high in the air, while all around him, white patches appeared and rocks showed through as the tide went out.

The dinghy slewed broadside on into the surf, lifted high and smashed down against a great green slab of rock. Brady disappeared over the stern into a cauldron of boiling water.

He tried to stand up. All around him, boulders were appearing and disappearing as the waves foamed over them and then he was lifted with irresistible force and carried over the reef towards the base of the cliffs.

The water receded with a great sucking sound and he hooked his fingers into the gravel and forced himself to his knees.

He lurched forward, scrambling desperately over the rocks. A moment later, the water boiled waist-high again, tugging at his limbs with great curling fingers that tried to take him out to sea. He grabbed at a crevasse in a boulder and hung on.

As the water receded, he forced himself forward over the final line of jagged rocks. A moment later, he was safe on the narrow strip of beach at the base of the cliffs.

He sat down, holding his head in his hands, and the world spun away into the roaring of the sea and the taste of it was in his throat and he retched, bringing up a great quantity of salt water.

After a while he got to his feet and turned to examine the cliffs behind him. They were no more than seventy or eighty feet high and sloped gently backwards, cracked and fissured with great gullies.

It was an easy enough climb, but he was tired—very tired. The sea still roared in his ears and there was an element of unreality to everything as if none of this were really happening to him.

What am I doing here? he asked himself. There was no answer. No answer at all and he hauled himself over the edge of the cliff and sprawled face down in the wet grass.

(12)

AFTER a while he opened his eyes and saw the boots a few inches from his face. They were hand-made and very expensive. He started to get up and there was a low, warning growl like thunder rumbling faintly in the distance.

He rolled on to his back and looked up. Miklos Davos stood over him. He wore a thigh-length hunting jacket with a fur collar and a green Tyrolean hat slanted across the wedge-shaped devil's face. He carried a double-barrelled shotgun under one arm.

The source of the growl was a magnificent black-and-tan Dobermann and it moved forward threateningly, eyes glowing like hot coals.

"Down, Kurt! Down!" Davos said. "I don't think we need to worry about Mr. Brady. He doesn't look too healthy."

He squatted, the shotgun comfortably across his

knees, and produced a large leather hip flask. "I've been watching your progress for the past half-hour. You've had a rough crossing. A little brandy will settle your stomach."

Brady didn't bother to argue. He took the flask and swallowed, coughing as the raw liquor burned its way down into his gullet.

A warm, pleasant glow spread inside him. He swallowed deeply again and began to feel a little better.

Davos had busied himself lighting a Turkish cigarette and now he smiled. "I trust you feel less like a corpse, my friend."

"You lousy bastard!" Brady croaked.

A slight sardonic smile touched the dark, saturnine face. "So, there is still a spark of life? That promises very well. Would you care for a cigarette?"

Brady took one and leaned forward for the proffered light. For a moment, he considered making a move, but as if sensing his thoughts, the Dobermann growled threateningly.

Brady subsided, coughing slightly as the smoke of the harsh Turkish tobacco caught at the back of his throat, and Davos said, "By the way, as I haven't heard from Haras since yesterday, I'm presuming I won't do."

"I'm afraid he met with a nasty accident last night," Brady said. "He should have looked where he was going."

"You've really done astonishingly well during the last couple of days," Davos said. "When Haras told me you'd somehow got out of Manningham Gaol and given him the slip, I had a premonition we would see each other again."

"I'd have followed you to Hell if necessary," Brady said.

"But Hell is too crowded, my friend." Davos smiled gently. "There was never anything of a personal nature in this affair, Brady."

"I know," Brady said wearily. "I just happened to be the first drunk on the first bench on the Embankment that night."

"I'm afraid you were," Davos said. "If they had carried out the death sentence, everything would have been fine. Unfortunately, the Home Secretary chose to commute it to life imprisonment."

"That must have really messed things up for you," Brady said.

"It did, I assure you," Davos said. "In this country reprieved murderers serve on the average, no more than seven years of their sentence. The English are such a humane people."

"So you decided to carry out the original sentence of the court," Brady said.

"I had no choice." Davos shrugged. "There was always the chance that you would see my face somewhere and recognize it. Perhaps the odd newspaper photo or something like that. If not this year, the next or the one after. I had no intention of allowing such a possibility to threaten my peace of mind indefinitely."

Brady flicked his cigarette out into space. He was tired. So tired that he was finding it difficult to concentrate. "What happens now?"

"An intriguing situation, isn't it?" Davos smiled. "Just the two of us—and Kurt, of course. I sent my caretaker and his wife over to the mainland when I arrived yesterday."

The Hungarian stood up and Brady scrambled to his feet and faced him, swaying slightly. "What's it to be? A bullet in the back?"

"But my dear fellow, nothing so unsporting." Davos patted the dog and it whined restlessly. "Wonderful animals, Dobermanns, Brady. When fully trained, they can kill a man in under a minute."

"Quite an accomplishment," Brady said.

"It is indeed." Davos backed away and raised the shotgun. "I think the fence at the top of the slope would give you a fair start. It must be at least seventy-five yards away."

"I'd like about two minutes alone with you," Brady said bitterly. "That's all it would take."

"I suggest you get started," Davos said. "My patience is beginning to run out."

Brady took his time going up the slope. There was no strength left in him and his limbs felt as heavy as lead.

He paused once to glance back over his shoulder. Davos stood waiting, holding the dog firmly by its collar. "You'll have to do better than that, Brady," he called.

What had the woman called him? *A brutal and perverted sadist, ceaselessly searching for new sensation.* Something sparked inside Brady, filling him with white-hot killing rage, flooding his weary limbs with a new energy. He breasted the slope in a few quick strides and clambered over the fence.

The Dobermann howled once as Davos released it and Brady ran down a slight incline into a wooded valley. At most, he had three or four minutes. He ran

(153)

into the trees and blundered through a plantation of young firs, branches slashing his face.

He staggered on, one arm raised as a shield and suddenly lost his balance and fell, rolling over and over down a bank through sodden bracken and into a small stream.

It was no more than a couple of feet deep and he followed its course for thirty or forty yards, brown water foaming around him as he splashed forward, until the water deepened suddenly as the stream emptied into a round pool.

He struggled across to the other side and pulled himself up out of the water on to a steeply shelving bank, covered with boulders and rocks.

Somewhere near by, the Dobermann howled and he could hear it crashing through the undergrowth. He started to peel his sodden jacket from his body. He had just got it off, when the dog erupted from the undergrowth on the far side of the pool, plunged into the water and swam strongly towards him.

He waited until it was about three feet away and tossed his jacket over its head. The Dobermann reared up, snarling and trying to free itself and Brady picked up a stone as big as a man's head, staggered into the water and brought it down with all his force.

There was a dreadful cracking sound and bone splintered. The Dobermann screamed like a human being and bucked frantically. He brought the stone down again and all movement ceased.

He turned away, sobbing for breath and scrambled across the slippery boulders. Now all he had to do was stay ahead of Davos and get to the house. There was bound to be another gun there somewhere.

He could taste blood in his mouth as he clawed his way up through the fir trees and emerged on to level ground. At this point, the trees swept out in an arc, thinly scattered over the ground, until they almost touched the fence. As Brady started forward, there was a cry of anger and Davos appeared about forty yards to the left.

The Hungarian moved with astonishing rapidity, firing the first barrel as he ran. Brady was almost at the fence. He ducked as shot screamed through the rain over his head and then scrambled over and started to run, weaving desperately from side to side.

He had gone no more than twenty yards when the Hungarian reached the fence and fired the second barrel. Brady cried out in agony, tripped and rolled over and over, stopping a little way from the edge of the cliffs, his face to the sky, a stone digging painfully into his back.

The main blast had missed him, but several pellets had caught him in the left shoulder and arm and he sat up, his face grey with pain as blood soaked through his sleeve.

Davos moved down the slope towards him and halted five or six feet away. His face was white with rage and a muscle twitched convulsively in his jaw.

"I can forgive you many things, Brady," he said, "but not the dog. Not Kurt."

A helicopter swung in from the sea about a quarter of a mile away, its fuselage a vivid yellow smudge against the grey sky. The sound of its engine had no meaning for Davos. He broke open the shotgun and took two fresh cartridges from his breast pocket, his eyes never leaving Brady's face.

The stone upon which Brady had come to rest was about the size of a tennis ball. His right hand fastened over it and he dashed it into the Hungarian's face with all his force.

It caught him in the right eye. He screamed and dropped the gun and Brady scrambled to his feet and flung himself forward. Davos, maddened by the pain of his damaged eye, swung out wildly and caught Brady full in the mouth.

Pain had no meaning for Brady and he bored in, forgetting his damaged left arm, forgetting everything except the one fixed idea of smashing Davos into the ground.

Davos clubbed him in the side of the neck and then Brady was in close. He lifted his right knee into the Hungarian's crotch and then into the face. Davos twisted as he fell and rolled over the edge of the cliff, sliding on his back down the rock slope to the beach.

Brady had no more strength left. He sat there in the grass and fought for breath as the helicopter hovered briefly at the top of the slope and landed.

When the door opened, the first man out was a police constable and after him, came Inspector Mallory holding his Homburg hat on with one hand as he moved out under the swinging blades.

Brady didn't wait to argue. He turned and went over the cliff feet-first, slipping and sliding down the slope in a shower of stones and tumbled into a heap of sand.

Davos was staggering along the shoreline towards the spur of rock which jutted out into the sea, separating them from the next cove. Brady scrambled to his feet and went after him.

The Hungarian heard him coming. He turned to glance over his shoulder and then plunged wearily into the sea and waded out to round the spur.

When Brady caught up with him, they were waist-deep in water. Davos had no fight left in him at all. He gave a strangled cry and thrashed wildly at the water as Brady seized him by the throat with both hands.

"You're going to tell them, you bastard!" Brady screamed. "You're going to tell them everything."

There was a strange roaring in his ears and he pressed down. The Hungarian's battered face disappeared beneath the water and then strong arms were pulling him away and Mallory was shouting in his ear, "It's all right, Brady. We know everything."

The inspector was standing beside him, the skirts of his raincoat billowing out in the water, somehow looking faintly ridiculous. Two constables supported Davos between them.

Mallory took Brady by the arm and led the way to the shore. They crossed the narrow strip of beach and Brady slumped down in the shelter of a large boulder. He was utterly spent, but his mind was crystal clear.

Mallory crouched beside him and examined his arm. "This looks pretty nasty. From the look of you, you could do with a couple of weeks in hospital."

"Never mind that," Brady said. "Tell me how you found out about Davos."

"Your friend, Miss Dunning, got in touch with me at about five o'clock this morning when she found you'd cleared out."

"And you believed her?"

Mallory shook his head. "She only gave me food for thought. I was still with her when I got a call from

Guy's Hospital. I'd had a man sitting at the bedside of Mrs. Rose Gordon, waiting for her to regain consciousness."

"But Haras shot her in the head," Brady said stupidly. "I was there."

"He only creased her," Mallory told him. "She made a most interesting statement. I got on to the R.A.F. at once."

"The helicopter was a nice touch."

Mallory grinned. "They picked us up at the South Bank landing stage. I wanted to get here fast. My one fear was that you might have done for Davos before we arrived."

Stones rattled down in a fine spray. As Brady glanced up Anne Dunning slid the last few feet down to the beach. She wore a belted raincoat and headscarf and her face was white and drawn.

Mallory stood up. "I'll help them get Davos up top. We'll come back for you in a few minutes."

He moved away and the girl came forward and crouched down beside Brady. She removed her headscarf and started to tie it about his arm and shoulder.

"You shouldn't have left without telling me," she said.

"There was nothing else I could do," he told her. "Don't forget, I thought Mrs. Gordon was dead. In any case, I didn't want to involve you any further. Things didn't look too good."

She smoothed the hair back from his brow. "You look as if you've had a bad time."

"It's all over now," he said. "And that's the main thing. Got a cigarette?"

She produced a crumpled pack and lit one for him.

As she passed it across, she said hesitantly, "What are you going to do now?"

"Boston, I think," he said. "And that job my brother-in-law offered me. I've had England for the time being."

She looked out to sea, pain on her face, and he slipped an arm around her shoulders. "Is that okay with you?"

She turned sharply, sudden tears in her eyes. "Damn you, Matt Brady. I thought you weren't going to ask me."

He pulled her close against his chest and somewhere high in the sky, a seagull cried harshly and dipped low over their heads before flying out to sea.